I0601577

SLEEPY DEATH

Sleepy Death

A Patrick Dawlish Mystery

**John Creasey *writing as*
Gordon Ashe**

INTEGRATED MEDIA
NEW YORK

All rights reserved, including without limitation the right to reproduce this book or any portion thereof in any form or by any means, whether electronic or mechanical, now known or hereinafter invented, without the express written permission of the publisher.

This is a work of fiction. Names, characters, places, events, and incidents either are the product of the author's imagination or are used fictitiously. Any resemblance to actual persons, living or dead, businesses, companies, events, or locales is entirely coincidental.

Copyright © 1953 by John Creasey

ISBN: 978-1-5040-9874-8

This edition published in 2025 by Open Road Integrated Media, Inc.
180 Maiden Lane
New York, NY 10038
www.openroadmedia.com

SLEEPY DEATH

CHAPTER I

WELCOME HOME

She wasn't so much beautiful as charming. She was small, dark and nicely made, and wore clothes which had come from Mayfair or Paris. There was a look of quicksilver about her, of vitality. She walked to and fro across the station, obviously impatient, and kept looking at the clock. She behaved as if no one else were at Victoria, although thirty or forty people were waiting for the arrival of the Golden Arrow from Paris, including several Cooks' men and agents from other travel agencies.

The Golden Arrow was ten minutes late, belying its reputation as one of the most punctual trains in England.

Several men, being men, watched the girl. One was large and ungainly to look at; most would have thought him ugly. He had untidy dark hair and big features, large eyes partly covered by drooping lids, and he wore a dark brown suit which needed pressing. He did not appear to take much notice of the girl, but probably he observed more than anyone else; he was sure that she was on edge and thought it was partly due to fear.

The girl stopped a porter.

"Is it never coming?"

"Won't be long now, miss." The porter looked at her and even his dull life was brightened. He smiled. "Five minutes, at the most."

"Thank you."

She turned away.

The big, ungainly man was able to admire her profile. He saw her head lift sharply, as she caught sight of someone coming into the station. She stared—and the big man looked to see who had caught her eye.

It was a man.

He was neither short nor tall, was well-dressed and sleek. He was smiling. It wasn't a pleasant or reassuring smile. Gloating? It was as if he were getting pleasure out of someone else's pain.

The big man was not close enough to see the expression in the girl's eyes, but he saw her turn away. The sleek man made a beeline for her. Before he reached her, she quickened her pace. She made for an exit, and didn't glance back. The sleek man frowned, but his smile didn't fade altogether; he was very sure of himself as he walked after the girl.

The big man followed, walking with a pronounced limp but making good pace. When he reached the booking-hall, both man and girl had disappeared; if he wanted to find them he would have to leave the station. He stood watching for a few minutes, then shrugged and turned back to the crowd waiting for the Golden Arrow. It was much larger, now, but no longer seemed the same crowd. Some of the life had been drawn out of it.

Patrick Dawlish and his wife, Felicity, sat opposite each other in a compartment of the Golden Arrow as it roared through Clapham Junction station, scornful of London's drab grey roofs of nearer suburbia. Dawlish, a very large man, with corn-coloured hair and good features except for a broken nose, looked at Felicity unsmilingly. His expression was blank, his cornflower blue eyes were dull.

"Clapham Junction," said Felicity. "Now we shan't be long."

Dawlish stirred. "Eh?"

"Clapham Junction," repeated Felicity.

"Oh, yes." He beamed, and turned his head. "So it was. Well, well, Now we shan't be long."

His wife frowned.

"Darling," she said.

"Yes, dear?"

"What's on your mind?"

"A beautiful woman."

"I'm not surprised. You haven't given me a minute's attention for the last hour."

"Too engrossed," said Dawlish. "Too far gone. How on earth do you do it?"

"Put up with you? I don't know," said Felicity, with feeling. "I must have been given a special gift of patience. Goodness knows, I need it."

"Unkind," reproached Dawlish. The train slowed down, and a little green electric suburban train roared past impertinently. "But I forgive you. I feel very kindly towards you, and full of admiration. How many women could spend ten days in Paris, stay up until three o'clock most nights, go gadding about by day, try on about a hundred models and be fussed and fiddled with by Paris dressmakers for ages, then finish a twelve-hour train journey and look as fresh and lovely as you? Don't tell me the secret, let me revel in mystery."

Felicity laughed.

"Fool. Bless you!"

"I'll have you know I speak only the truth. You don't look a day older than when I first met you."

Felicity smiled; loving all this.

"In fact," said Dawlish, "I've been pondering over various aspects of this phenomenon for the past hour."

"I know *that's* a lie," said Felicity. "Don't spoil it. Darling—"

"Yes?"

"You did enjoy yourself, didn't you?"

"It was gorgeous."

"Be serious."

"I couldn't be more serious. I love champagne, even at four thousand francs a bottle. I love the night clubs, too; there's no place in the world like Paris." Dawlish grinned. "You must take me there again one day. I wouldn't be safe without a chaperone."

"At least I know that," said Felicity. "Well, here we are." She leaned forward, and Dawlish kissed her cheek. "It'll be nice to be home again."

"Ah," said Dawlish. "Still no place like it. Sure you feel up to the car journey tonight? We could stay in town; there's always room at Tim's, and then drive down in the morning."

"I wouldn't keep you away from your apples and pigs for another five minutes, for anything in the world," said Felicity.

They were running into the station, passing porters eager and ready to take luggage. It was characteristic of Dawlish that he didn't stand up until the train had stopped—and normal that a porter should be waiting for the crook of his little finger. Three minutes later they were walking behind the porter as he trundled his trolley and their five suit-cases towards the barrier. They were halfway along the train, and the seething mass beyond the barrier was in constant motion.

Their car was garaged a few hundred yards away.

"I'll go and get the car, you wait with the luggage," Dawlish said. "I won't be long."

"All right, darling."

They were through the barrier, and Dawlish took two long steps towards the exit when he heard his name called. "*Pat!*" He looked round. Felicity, only a yard behind, was staring towards the caller.

He was the big, untidy man who had observed so much.

"Well, would you believe it?" demanded Dawlish of Felicity. "Ted's come to welcome us home." They went together and joined Edward Beresford—and side by side the men looked like giants in a race of pigmies; Felicity, although tall for a woman, was a head shorter than Dawlish. She had to look up at Beresford, as he took her hand; her expression was undoubtedly tinged with suspicion.

"Now this," said Dawlish, "is friendly of you. We've just about time for a quick one, too. Fel's anxious to get home tonight, and—"

"*I'm* anxious!" exclaimed Felicity.

"You can't get back soon enough to find out how much dust has accumulated since you left and whether Bessie's had a major disaster with the china." Dawlish squeezed her arm. "Hallo, Ted. How's Joan? Infants? Everyone?"

"Fine."

"Good." They were walking together now, and the porter with the trolley followed them.

Beresford, who had a deep voice, said, "I suppose you must go down to Haslemere tonight."

"There's no compulsion," Dawlish said. "Why?"

"I'd like a chat," said Beresford airily. "Supposing we go to Tim's flat? He's out, but he'll be back later. He'd like to see you, too."

Dawlish looked down at his wife. She shook her head slowly, and the suspicion in her eyes was more marked.

"Home," she said.

"You heard," said Dawlish severely. "We must go home. The dust can't wait."

Beresford mumbled.

"Oh, well. Can't be helped, I suppose." He looked unhappy. "Can't say I blame Fel. On the other hand, I think you ought to hear all about this. Odd business."

"We don't want to hear anything about any odd business," declared Felicity. "Pat, you hound, you know something about this. That's what you were thinking about in the train. Own up."

"Not true."

"I'll bet it is!"

"He couldn't have known anything about it," said Beresford firmly. "I didn't know myself until last night, and wasn't sure that it was anything worth worrying about until this morning. So I had a word with Tim."

"Damn Tim!" said Felicity, with feeling.

"Tell you what," said Dawlish, as if inspired, "you two wait here while I go and get the car."

He didn't give Felicity a chance to argue, but turned and hurried off. The porter looked from him to Felicity, and scratched his head. Felicity stared after him until he was out of sight, and then looked back at Beresford.

"Just leave it here," Beresford said.

"What?"

"Not you, Fel. The porter," said Beresford hastily. "Come back in a quarter of an hour."

"Right, sir."

Beresford beamed at Felicity and pointed to the five suit-cases, four of which were large ones, and asked ingenuously, "Have any trouble with customs?"

"Never mind Customs." Felicity sounded angry. "Why on

earth did you have to do this, Ted? It's too bad. It's bad enough when Pat's in England and gets mixed up in mystery, but when you and Tim get involved in something and then have to wait for him to pull you out of the mess, it's—"

"Too bad," said Beresford forlornly. "I know. Still, Pat will be Pat. Don't blame me for what he is. Everything would be all right if he'd become a policeman, then it would just be his job."

"Well, it isn't his job."

Beresford smiled broadly at her. Smiling, he wasn't ugly. His eyes smiled, too, as he pressed her arm.

"Sometimes it must be hell to be married to him. I know. On the other hand, Fel, he really has a flare for detection. He's never come off second best, either. Being Pat, you wouldn't want him to stand by if he could lend a useful hand. I think he can, this time. As a matter of fact, I had a word with Bill Trivett this morning. Went along to Scotland Yard to see him. I put a theoretical case to him. An old man who moves in highest circles, being blackmailed. As simple as that, actually, but with one unusual slant. I wasn't to divulge the victim's name to the police, but could name the blackmailer. Directly I did, Bill said it was a job for Pat."

Felicity did not thaw.

"That's the Yard all over. If they can't do a thing themselves, they expect Pat to do it. Who is the old man? Why should Pat help him? Give me one good reason?"

Beresford still smiled, but more gently.

The old man's worth helping, I think. The blackmailer's made hell for him. The police have been after this particular black-mailer for years and haven't been able to get him. They think Pat might. Pat isn't restricted as to method. You know," Beresford went on, "this isn't one of the big shows, it's simple and human, and I think you'd be sorry if you stopped Pat from taking it up."

"Blarney," said Felicity. "Anyhow, you know perfectly well that I couldn't stop Pat if he'd made up his mind to do a thing. I suppose we'll have to come to Tim's. Why Tim's place, anyhow?"

"The old man's there, waiting to see the great Dawlish," said Beresford.

'The Great Dawlish' strode along the Vauxhall Bridge Road towards the garage, and most people who noticed him would have suspected that his brains had been lost in brawn. He looked wooden-faced and dull. He took no apparent interest in anyone. He did not even wonder why Ted Beresford had thought anything urgent enough to meet him.

It was more than ten years since he had first become a national figure because of his peculiar flare for a particular brand of two-fisted detection; he still marvelled that anyone singled him out from the crowd.

Superintendent William Trivett of the Yard, a long-headed policeman who seldom had patience with amateurs, had been heard to say that Dawlish must have a sixth sense. Whereat Dawlish had laughed.

As he walked, thinking mostly of Felicity, something happened to Dawlish. He passed hundreds of people, dozens of buses, as many taxis and more private cars, without really noticing them, yet he 'noticed' that he was being followed, although he hadn't consciously looked at the man. He simply knew that he was being followed; so obviously, the next step was to find out who it was.

CHAPTER II

ACTION

The garage was in a narrow *cul-de-sac*, and the turning off the main road was marked on one side by a telephone kiosk and on the other by a café; not the kind of café which Dawlish would frequent by choice. He didn't enter now. He turned the corner, and actually began to whistle.

Two oil-daubed mechanics were tinkering with a little M.G. roadster outside the garage, which was small, but run by a man who had genius in everything concerning internal combustion. Dawlish always had his car serviced there when in London. There was a row of lock-up garages next to the workshop, and Dawlish went straight to one, nodding to the mechanics, who stopped work to nod back.

He unlocked his door.

His black Rolls-Bentley glowed at him. He patted the nose, as he might a horse, climbed in, fiddled and, two minutes later, drove the car out of the garage and pulled up beside the petrol pump.

The mechanics stopped again and a small lad in dirty overalls came up leisurely.

"'Morning, sir."

"Hallo, Joe. Fill her up, will you? Everything else been checked?"

"All okeydoke, sir."

"Good." Dawlish nodded, leaned against the front of the car and lit a cigarette. For the first time he looked for the man who had been following him. Several men were crossing the end of the road; only one loitered. He was short, dressed in a draught-board yellow-and-black sports jacket and a pair of flannel trousers, and wore a trilby hat with a large brim which was pulled low over his forehead and hid his eyes. There were probably several replicas of him in London. He showed no outward interest in Dawlish, but was looking his way. Casually he turned and disappeared.

The two mechanics had returned to their tinkering and the boy was setting the pump. None of them saw Dawlish move. The boy said:

"How many do you think she'll take, sir?"

There was no reply, and he stared—and gaped. Dawlish was at the corner; he'd reached it so quickly that he might have taken a flying leap.

"Cor!" gasped the boy. "See that?"

The mechanics only saw Dawlish disappearing round the corner.

The man with the draught-board jacket was in the telephone kiosk. Dawlish flattened himself against the wall and moved his head so that he could see a flat-tipped forefinger in the dialling-hole. He stretched out his hand and opened the door a fraction of an inch as the man said:

"Percy?"

Presumably Percy answered, for he went on in a hoarse voice:

"He's here. Picked up a whacking great car, Rolls-Bentley. Black, number—" He gave the number, and paused. "I can try, but it wants an aeroplane to keep up with a thing like that . . . okay."

He rang off.

Had he glanced round a moment earlier he would have seen Dawlish. As it was, only passers-by saw the giant, and were staring in surprise at his peculiar behaviour. Dawlish now stood against the wall, cigarette drooping from his lips. The other came out of the kiosk, glanced up and down—and saw Dawlish. His jaw dropped.

"Hallo," said Dawlish. "How's Percy?"

The man's jaw dropped lower; much lower.

"I'll have to meet him myself one day," murmured Dawlish. "We're going for a little walk. Come along." He stretched out his hand, and the other was so mesmerised that he didn't try to get free before it was too late. Fingers with a grip like a vice closed over his forearm, and he was pulled towards Dawlish with a force he couldn't resist. Close together they turned the corner.

"I shall now call a policeman," said Dawlish firmly.

"I—I ain't done nothing!"

"I seem to have heard that phrase before." Dawlish beamed. "As a matter of fact, you don't know it, but you stole my wallet. That's what I shall tell the policeman, and he'll take you away and lock you up. How's your reputation? Can it stand half an hour at Scotland Yard?"

The man gulped.

"Somehow I didn't think it would," said Dawlish. "Of course, there's a way of avoiding it. You can tell me where I'll find Percy, and what his other name is, and if you don't lie, I'll forget the policeman." They were now approaching the garage, and the boy and the two mechanics stared. Except that Dawlish had his hand on his captive's wrist, there now seemed nothing unusual.

"You—you've got me wrong, mister, I—"

"I can find out without much trouble," said Dawlish. "If I ask Scotland Yard to weigh in, they'll do it for me. And you'll be cooling your heels in a cell. Please yourself. Who is Percy and where does he live?"

The man drew a deep breath, looked into Dawlish's eyes, seemed to realize that he hadn't a chance of getting away, and muttered:

"He'll carve you to pieces. He—"

"Nice chap. Percy who?"

"Dipper. Percy Dipper, he—"

"Address?"

"Twenty-one, Mill Street, Chelsea, but he—"

"Will carve me to pieces, I heard you the first time," said Dawlish. "Someone will have to stick me together again. Listen, little one. You're going to cool your heels in my garage. If you've told me the truth you'll be released, if you've lied you'll see the police." He still had the key to the lock-up, and reached it, watched by the trio from the garage. "It's nice and clean," he said soothingly, "and you'll soon get used to the smell of oil." He thrust the man in, closed the door and turned the key; then smilingly he faced the trio. The boy hastily started the petrol pump.

"I'll need the garage for a few hours," said Dawlish. "Don't let him out, and if he makes any fuss, call a copper. All ready for me?"

The boy's eyes glowed.

"Won't be half a jiff, Mr. Dawlish."

"Thanks." Dawlish got into the car again, waited until the

tank was filled, and drove off. Five minutes later he pulled up alongside Felicity and Beresford, the porter and their luggage. Felicity no longer looked contented; her eyes stormed.

"You aren't just beautiful, you're superb," Dawlish said.

"Where on *earth* have you been?"

"Sorry," Dawlish said, and smiled inanely. "Had a little trouble. Ted, get a cab, and take Fel to the flat. I'll be there later." He blew Felicity a kiss, and drove off, well out of earshot before she could speak. When he glanced round he saw that she had recovered the power of speech and that Ted Beresford was developing a long-suffering look. He drove on—and forgot Felicity. That was the kind of thing Felicity hated most; on a case, he was capable of forgetting even her.

Mill Street, Chelsea, was not in the artists' quarter nor in one of the better residential neighbourhoods. The houses were small and in long terraces; at each corner a general shop sold everything from newspapers to needles and offered tips and guides to racing form. Not far off the giant chimneys of the Lots Road power station showed dark against the evening sky. In half an hour it would be quite dark. Lights showed at some of the windows, and as Dawlish drove past he was several at Number 21.

There seemed to be no difference between Number 21 and all the other little houses. The front door opened straight on to the pavement, the woodwork needed painting and there were curtains at the windows. Dawlish drove to the corner and turned, knowing that the dozen or so people in the street were watching his car; Rolls-Bentleys seldom came so far off the beaten track.

At the corner was a pub—the King's Arms. Dawlish left the car outside, winked at two urchins who stood by the saloon door, and said:

"Keep an eye on it for me, will you?"

"*Okay*, mister!" They were enthusiastic.

"Thanks." Dawlish walked round the corner and along the narrow street, watched from a dozen windows. He wasn't sure whether he was watched from that of Number 21. He reached it, and knocked—a single loud knock which reverberated up and down the street.

He lit another cigarette.

After a moment or two, footsteps sounded inside; shuffling, unsteady. He stood to one side until the door began to open. Then he stepped forward swiftly, put a foot against the door, and smiled at the old man who stood there.

"'Oo—"

"I want a word with Percy," said Dawlish. He put a hand on the old man's arm and moved him aside, went into a narrow passage, smelt stale cabbage and tobacco smoke—and heard a door slam upstairs. The old man muttered a protest which Dawlish hardly noticed. He strode down the narrow passage which ran alongside the stairs. The smell of cabbage grew stronger. He thrust open a door which led to a kitchen. An old woman was sitting in a wicker chair, nodding, greasy grey hair drooping down her neck to her shoulders, a pair of steel-rimmed glasses on her nose.

"Good evening," said Dawlish.

There was another door on the right, leading to the back garden. It wasn't locked. He opened it and stepped into the cemented yard. Light streamed out from a window above—and the figure of a man showed, as if the man were climbing out of the window. Dawlish looked up. The man was actually out, and lowering himself carefully. He hadn't glanced down to see Dawlish.

He dropped lightly.

"Percy, I presume," said Dawlish, and gripped him round the waist. "Going places?"

He heard the man gasp and felt him wriggle. Then he saw his right hand move. He was quick, but Percy was quicker; a knife glinted, then moved in a vicious upward thrust towards Dawlish's side. Dawlish simply tightened his grip on the thin waist; the breath was crushed out of the man's body, the knife dropped, Percy gave a sighing gasp.

Dawlish slackened his hold, bent down and picked up the knife and slipped it into his pocket.

"You must be Percy. You measure up to all I've heard about him," he said. "You're not having a good night. We're going for a little walk."

Percy Dipper didn't answer; probably that was because he hadn't much breath left. Dawlish took his right arm and thrust him into the kitchen. The old man and the old woman were both there now, the woman standing; a frail old couple who looked terrified. Dawlish smiled at them but didn't speak, just helped Percy along the passage. The front door was closed. He opened it.

"What—?" began Percy, and stopped.

"We'll talk later," said Dawlish. "Just do as you're told or you'll get hurt."

In those few minutes the night had become much darker, street lamps and lights from windows showed more clearly, and fell upon the faces of thirty or forty people who had gathered round. Most were ordinary faces, here and there one had a vicious look. Several of the men were undoubtedly friends of Percy, but no one spoke and no one tried to interfere. Dawlish forced his way through the crowd, still holding Percy tightly, and reached the corner. The boys were keeping faithful watch over the car.

"Strewth!" one gasped.

"Life's full of surprises," said Dawlish brightly. "I'm going to take Percy for a ride. If anyone wants to know where he's gone, tell them that he's with Dawlish. Patrick Dawlish. That'll be all they'll want to know." He tossed a two-shilling piece towards the nearer urchin. "Split that."

He let Percy go—and then struck him beneath the chin, a short-arm jab which snapped Percy's teeth together. He smiled all the time as he opened the door, lifted Percy and dumped him on the seat, then went to the driving door. Ten minutes after he had arrived at Mill Street he was driving towards the main road. This time he was watched by scores of staring eyes, not all of them hostile.

Timothy Jeremy's flat was in a mews almost equidistant from Oxford Street and Park Lane. It was a quiet spot. On dark nights it was almost possible to walk over the cobbles on the road and picture the scene as it had been two hundred years ago, lighted by flares, with link-boys standing about and coachmen preparing horses and carriage for their master's pleasure. By day, the red tiles of the roofs of the old stables showed the green of lichen. The stables themselves had been turned into lock-up garages, and the rooms above, once servants' quarters, into flats. There were two flats, each approached by a flight of cement steps, incongruous against the old brick walls and the gabled windows.

Dawlish turned beneath the brick archway which led to the mews. A single electric light glowed in one corner, shining on the doors of the garages. One was empty, which meant that Tim was out in his car. That didn't surprise Dawlish, but the fact that there were no lights at the windows astonished him. Felicity and Ted ought to have been here half an hour ago.

He sat at the wheel, with Percy conscious and frightened by his side; and he felt the first twinges of disquiet.

CHAPTER III

CHAT WITH PERCY

Dawlish forced the disquiet down, got out, and went round to the other door of the car. Percy climbed out meekly, showing no inclination to run away. Dawlish pointed to the first of the cement stairways, which had a flimsy-looking wooden handrail.

"Up you go."

Percy obeyed; cringing.

Dawlish looked round and listened, but heard no car approaching. Had the others been delayed in getting a taxi? Had they needed one? Ted Beresford would almost certainly use his own car. Dawlish frowned, and followed Percy up the steps. He had a key, for this was a communal flat, although these days only Tim Jeremy was a permanent resident. Beresford seldom used it, and the Dawlishes found it not only a convenient *pied à terre*, but a hallowed spot; it had been their first home.

Everything was silent.

Dawlish opened the door and stepped in, behind Percy, found the light switch and pressed it down. Light flooded a narrow hall-passage. There were three doors, two of them closed; the third, the kitchen door, stood wide open.

"That way." He pointed to the kitchen door.

Percy moved forward. Dawlish looked at the other two doors, and shook his head. Had there been any light, he would have seen it from outside. One room was a bedroom, with a smaller bedroom leading off. The door leading to the kitchen also led to a small passage, and off this was a third, tiny bedroom and the bathroom. Percy stood in the doorway, not certain which way to go.

"Left," said Dawlish.

He wished Felicity were here; it worried him. Telling himself there was no need to worry didn't really help. He followed Percy into the tiny bedroom, seldom used, furnished simply and with good taste; Felicity's. Dawlish switched on the lights, which were concealed in the corners. Percy looked round, dazed and dazzled.

He had little to recommend him.

A small man with a long chin which tapered to a narrow point, small mouth, with the upper lip sinking in a little, as if his top teeth were missing, a long, thin nose and little dark eyes. His forehead was narrow and the hair grew low on it. He had a lot of nearly black hair, thick with a potent pomade and brushed straight back from a low, lined forehead. He wore a light brown suit with exaggerated shoulders and a wasp waist.

He had a bruise on the point of his chin; and his eyes were bloodshot.

"Sit down, Percy," said Dawlish, in a surprisingly mild voice.

Percy dropped willingly into a bedroom chair covered with flowered chintz.

"We'll clear up one little mystery," Dawlish said. "I heard your buddy telephone, dealt with him as I have you, got your address and came straight over. Simple, you see. Why was he watching the station for me?"

Percy licked his lips.

Dawlish said: "We won't waste any time, Percy, I'm in a hurry. Why?"

Percy narrowed his eyes, and sniffed.

Dawlish took the knife out of his pocket and examined it for the first time. It wasn't much of a thing—a cobbler's knife, with the small blade sharpened to a razor edge; a weapon to wound and cut, but not to kill. Knives like this were as popular as razors among Percy's crowd.

Dawlish felt the blade with his thumb.

"Ever felt it?"

Percy muttered, "I—I wouldn't have—"

"You would have cut me open, Percy. And I'll cheerfully do the same to you." Dawlish's expression was blank and his eyes were dull—and Percy shivered, as if he had never seen a man who frightened him so much. "Why did you watch for me?"

"I—had orders!" The words burst out.

"Who from?"

"I—I don't know, I—"

Dawlish shot out his right hand and slapped Percy across the face. Percy's head jolted to one side, he felt as if a horse had kicked him. Dawlish had put more power into the blow than he had meant, partly because Felicity wasn't here. Tears of pain sprang to Percy's eyes, he shrank back in his chair, as frightened of Dawlish's fists as of the knife.

"Who gave the orders?" Dawlish asked evenly.

"I dunno! I—I think—" Percy swallowed what he thought.

"Think hard and think fast," Dawlish advised.

"I dunno for sure. I got a 'phone message, I think—"

He couldn't get the name out. Just a little more violence would carry the necessary persuasion. Dawlish bunched his fists.

"Nick Mascatti!" The name burst out like a champagne cork. "I dunno for certain, but I done a lot of jobs for him. I don't ask no questions." Percy was mumbling, but couldn't get the words out quickly enough. "Nick's a hard man to work for. I just do as I'm told and ask no questions. It couldn't be no one else—Nick Mascatti."

"I'm looking forward to meeting Nick. Where does he live?"

"Soho. Runs a restaurant and night club, all on the up-and-up. Don't—don't tell him—"

"If he gave the order and knows you gave him away there'll be trouble, will there?" asked Dawlish.

"He'll—he'll give me hell!"

"I can't think of anything I'd like better. When did he tell you to watch for me?"

"S'afternoon. Telephoned me—well, *someone* did. Mascatti always uses a mouthpiece. Told me you was on the Golden Arrow, wanted to know if anyone met you and where you went. I put Scotty on to you. Scotty's good, I don't know how you made him talk. Scot—"

"You told me. He's cooling his heels. What's the name of this club?"

"The Golden Shoe. *You* know."

Dawlish had heard of, but never been to, the Golden Shoe, partly because its reputation was so innocuous that no one who knew his way about the West End would be tempted to go. It was a pale imitation of a Paris night club, most of its clients were from the provinces, and they were easily satisfied. He had not heard of Mascatti, as far as he could remember; Scotland Yard would know of him.

"How long have you been working for him?" Dawlish asked.

"Years."

"How many years?"

"Five," said Percy, and licked his lips. "No, six. That's it, six. He don't give himself away, but *I* know it's him."

"Anyone else like you work for him?"

"I think so. He tells me to use others, sunnines."

A car sounded in the road approaching the mews. Dawlish listened to it, while studying the comic misery on Percy's face. The car drew nearer and passed the entrance to the mews.

"What jobs do you do for your pal Nick?"

"He ain't no pal! It—it might be anything."

"Such as?"

"Such as tailing you from the station and reporting. I can't tell you no more, Mr. Dawlish." Percy was sweating; and there was fear in his eyes, because he wasn't sure that Dawlish would believe him. Dawlish was not even trying to judge how much of the story was true, he only knew that Percy was trying to make sure that he would pay Nick Mascatti a lot of attention.

"Do you work for Mascatti all the time?"

"*All* the time? 'Course I don't, I've got—I've got me own work."

He didn't elaborate and Dawlish didn't need him to. Percy Dipper was one of a dozen minor gang leaders in London; they seldom came much worse. He was a bad man in a little way, and if he hadn't yet seen the inside of jail he would one day.

Dawlish said, "Who else is watching me?"

"No one, Mr. Dawlish!" Percy leaned forward earnestly. "There wasn't no reason why I should use anyone else; Scotty's good, I just had to report where you went, that's all."

"Did Mascatti's mouthpiece tell you where he expected me to go?"

"No, he never said a word. He never says anything more than he has to, Mr. Dawlish. There ain't another thing I can tell you. What—what's it worth to let me go?"

Dawlish actually laughed.

"You wait a bit, Percy. Go over to that cupboard." A wardrobe cupboard was built into the wall. Percy glanced round miserably, got up, and did as he was told. "Open the door," said Dawlish. Percy obeyed; the wardrobe cupboard was empty. "Step inside," ordered Dawlish, "and I'll come and see you later."

"Mr. Dawlish—"

"Inside."

Percy obeyed again mutely. Dawlish sauntered across, closed the doors, and locked them. Percy didn't utter a sound as Dawlish dropped the key into his pocket, then turned towards the room door.

After an hour or two in there, brooding over the threat of going to the police, Percy might make some alterations in his story.

Dawlish stepped towards the front door—and heard another car. He stood still. He heard the gears change, and began to smile, for he recognized the note of Beresford's engine. He went briskly to the door, opened it, and saw headlights shining on the wall of the buildings opposite the archway. Beresford's car was nosed in, cautiously, and stopped at the foot of the steps.

Apart from the headlamps and the flat light, it was now pitch dark. Dawlish stood against the light from the passage, saw Felicity open the door and look up—and saw Beresford getting out on the other side. Beresford had an artificial leg, and often moved awkwardly.

"And where have you been drinking?" Dawlish called.

"Drinking!" exclaimed Felicity. She came up the steps, and the light showed the sparkle in her eyes. She wasn't beautiful, by ordinary standards, her features were too broad; but to Dawlish she had beauty and a great deal more. "I think Ted did it deliberately."

"Honestly, Fel—" called Beresford plaintively.

"I don't believe a word of it," said Felicity, and drew level with Dawlish. "He *says* that the engine failed. We've been stuck for nearly an hour, while he messed about. Then a man came from a garage and fixed it in two shakes. Ted could have done it, but he wanted you to get here first. You two have been plotting this for days."

"Wrong," said Dawlish, and kissed her on the cheek.

"Don't slobber over me!"

"No, dear."

"Honestly, Fel," said Beresford, halfway up the steps, "I couldn't do a thing about it. I never was any good at the innards of a car, you ought to know that."

"You never were any good at anything," snapped Felicity. "As for *you*." She withered Dawlish with a look. "If you hadn't gone chasing off we could have been here an hour ago, and if you hadn't listened to this great oaf, you could have been nearly home by now. I'm—I'm *furious*."

"Go and make a nice cup of tea," said Dawlish. "You'll feel better then."

"Tea!" cried Felicity.

She stormed in. Dawlish grinned at Beresford, who looked lugubrious and smiled wanly. Felicity opened one of the doors inside the flat and slammed it.

"Ho, Ted!" Dawlish boomed. "Plenty of beer in?"

"Er—yes. Of course." Beresford frowned. "I couldn't help it, for once. Spot of trouble in the pump, easy when you know how to fix it. Things would go wrong tonight. I was just winning her round."

"She'll be all right."

"I hope so. I didn't want you to get here first, anyhow, I wanted a word with you about the old boy." Beresford moved towards the door. "You don't know a thing about it, but I suppose you've managed to glean most of it, by now. How is he?"

Dawlish said, "Who?"

"The old boy."

They were in the hall, and filled it. Felicity was moving about in the main bedroom. Beresford's expression became strained and Dawlish looked owlish.

"*What* old boy?"

"Now look here," said Beresford, "it's bad enough without you making it worse. The old boy who was waiting here to see you, of course. Don't tell me you haven't had a chat."

"No one's here," said Dawlish. "That is—" He broke off, and strode towards the door of the living-room.

"Do you mean to tell me he wasn't here?" Beresford stood in the doorway as Dawlish pressed the switch.

The room was empty.

A small table was overturned, a glass stood on its side, and liquid on the polished wood shone faintly in the light.

CHAPTER IV

MISSING MAN

There were no other signs of a struggle; the overturned table and glass were enough. Beresford poked his fingers through his unruly hair. Dawlish stared down at the glass, and his face was blank, his eyes were dull.

He went to the front door, shone a torch on the lock, and saw no sign of scratches.

He went back to the room.

"His name's Kimble," said Beresford abruptly. "Sir Anthony Kimble. I expect it rings a bell. Big research man—medical research. Rates pretty high. Did a good job during the war on drugs to help ease pain and patching up badly wounded chaps. Knighthood after the war—a lot of people thought he ought to have had something more. Widower. Fairly well off. For some time he's been blackmailed. He suspects but can't be sure that his blackmailer is a man named Rutter. He didn't say what Rutter or anyone else has on him. He was pathetic. He went down to Haslemere to see you, and your girl, Bessie, gave him Tim's address. So he came here—last night was the first time.

"He wasn't really satisfied with us, and Tim suggested he

should come here and be waiting for you when you got back. Tim's off, after Rutter—trying to pick up some odds and ends. I guessed you and Fel would want to get home tonight, so I was at the station. Thought of sending a telegram to the train, you'd have got it at Dover, but I knew it would spoil Fel's trip. That's most of the story."

Dawlish was still looking down at the glass, and picturing the scene. The old man sitting there with a whisky-and-soda in his hands, the door opening—a struggle. Not much of a struggle. It was possible that he'd knocked the table over when he'd jumped up. It was remotely possible that he'd done that by accident and gone off on his own accord. Nothing could be taken for granted.

"What's the rest?" Dawlish asked.

"Well—I wasn't too happy about things, and happened to run into Bill Trivett last night, at the club. I had a word with him. Thought Scotland Yard might know something about it. Kimble didn't mind me naming Rutter, but made me promise not to name Kimble himself to anyone but you. The name Rutter meant plenty to Trivett." Beresford smiled faintly. "Bad man they can't catch, quoth he, just your piece of cake. Thirsty?"

"I couldn't think why you were waiting."

Beresford went to a cupboard and took out two bottles of beer, two glasses and a bottle opener. The cupboard was old and of beautifully carved oak, black with centuries of polishing. The large room was obviously a bachelor's; the furniture was heavy, the armchairs large, most of the pictures were sporting prints; a set of golf clubs, a cricket bat and two tennis racquets were in a corner.

Beresford poured out.

"Nice head," he said. "Cheers."

They drank, as if it were a ritual.

"Ah," said Dawlish. "English beer again. Why can't they make it as good in France? Kimble really seemed worried, you say."

"Frightened."

"How long's he been paying blackmail?"

"Two years or so—he says."

"And now he's started trying to do something about it—I wonder why."

Beresford shrugged.

"Sure he was frightened, and not just tired of paying out the money?"

Beresford sat on the arm of a chair large enough for him; and that meant it was a mammoth chair. He pushed his hair back from his forehead, and looked sombre, almost ugly. His blue eyes were fixed on Dawlish intently. He measured his words.

"Pat, I'm not soft-hearted. Nor is Tim. But Kimble did something to us. We had exactly the same reaction. Here was a man in desperate trouble, and we just had to help him. I knew Fel wouldn't like it, knew it would have been wiser to let you settle in at Four Ways for a day or two, but I just couldn't wait. It's hard to say why. He was like a helpless child. Unworldly. Don't get me wrong now—not senile."

"Did he go or was he taken?" Dawlish asked mildly, and finished his beer.

"Take it from me, he wouldn't have left here willingly without seeing you. Someone sold you to him in a big way."

"His bad luck. Did he take precautions?"

"Closed car and reliable chauffeur. A hired car, too. He didn't take any chances."

"But if he was followed, he could as easily have been telephoned as called for," said Dawlish. "It begins to add up. After paying blackmail for years, the blackmailer tightens the squeeze and that puts a scare into Kimble. He can't go to the police so he comes to a private eye he's heard someone talking about.

The question is, what kind of squeeze? What does the black-mailer want that Kimble isn't prepared to pay? Just money?" He shrugged and moved towards the chair in which Kimble had been sitting. He felt down the sides of the cushion—and winced. When he drew his hand out a pin was sticking into the ball of the middle finger.

"Felicity's, or I'm a Dutchman," he said, and tried the other side. He whistled, and drew something else out, between his fore- and middle-finger. It was a wallet, a thin one of black leather.

"Lost anything?" he asked.

"Not mine." Beresford's voice was sharp. "Not Tim's, either."

"If Kimble knew they'd found him and wanted to get rid of this, it would be easy to slip this down the side of the chair," Dawlish said slowly. He drew out several visiting cards, all Kimble's, and a folded piece of thin paper—airmail paper, which crackled as he unfolded it slowly. It was covered on one side with writing, but Dawlish couldn't read it—the wording looked to be in Latin, and there were a great number of symbols. Beresford came across and looked.

"Medical mumbo jumbo," he pronounced.

"Could be what the others are after," said Dawlish, and replaced it carefully in the wallet. "I—"

The door opened abruptly, and Felicity came in. She had changed into an emerald green house-coat which she always kept at the flat. Her cheeks were flushed and her eyes were bright, and Dawlish liked the effect. She left the door wide open, and said with deceptive calmness:

"Are we going to leave the cases in the car all night for your light-fingered friends to take, or do you expect me to bring them up?"

"Hullo, my sweet!" cried Dawlish, as if she hadn't spoken.

He moved with his bewildering speed, reached her, placed his hands at her waist and lifted her. She was helpless. He raised her until her head almost touched the ceiling, and grinned up. "Look at her, Ted! I can still span her waist. I don't think she's put an inch on in ten years. What about that for feminine discipline and a life in the country?" He lowered her slowly, until their faces were level; and touched noses. "*I* will get the cases with my own fair hands. No others shall touch the latest models from Paris. How many are there? Four, isn't it? That *chic* little afternoon thing which has nothing to speak of in front, that purple, or is it mauve—"

"Let me down!"

"—evening gown, without a back, if I remember rightly. The suit—Ted, you should see her in that suit! It's not the last word, it won't be the last word until the year after next, it's that far ahead of fashion. And then—but I won't go on. I'd hate to tell you how many francs the ingenuous French dressmaker wormed out of us, but it will keep him from starvation for a decade or so."

He put Felicity lightly on the floor.

"He's gone," he said.

Felicity didn't speak.

"Did you tell her about Kimble?" Dawlish asked.

Beresford nodded.

"The nice old man's gone. Kidnapped, probably," said Dawlish. "Not bad work, when you come to think of it, Ted couldn't have been away more than an hour. A little more, perhaps—how long, Ted?"

"About two," said Beresford.

"And in that time they snooped in, snatched Kimble and vanished." Dawlish lit a cigarette. "I wish I knew where I could find him. Not a nice job, Fel, is it?"

Felicity said slowly: "Oh, I suppose you'll have to go on with

31

it, now it's started. But get the cases. I want to hang those dresses for the night."

"Two jiffs," promised Dawlish. "And what about that tea? Or would you care for a man's drink?"

"I'll make some tea." Felicity turned towards the kitchen.

"Food?" Beresford asked.

"We had early dinner on the train. You hungry?"

"I'll get a snack later," said Beresford. "We'll have those cases up in a couple of jiffs."

The two men went to the steps as Felicity went into the kitchen. Dawlish hesitated for a few seconds at the car, then took out one case and stood it on end; soon all five were there. He took two, carried them up, and heard Beresford following; Beresford could only manage one. Dawlish put his cases down at the top of the steps and examined the key-hole again. He frowned, then went in. Beresford joined him in the bedroom. They could hear Felicity humming in the kitchen, and Beresford grinned.

Dawlish said, "Ted, go and have a glance at the lock of the front door, will you?"

Beresford went off. When Dawlish joined him, he was studying the lock; when Dawlish had collected the two cases and brought them up, Beresford had finished.

"Well?" asked Dawlish heavily.

"No scratches, no damage."

"I was afraid I hadn't missed anything. They had a key."

"Could have been a neat job with a pick lock."

"Be yourself. You can't force that lock with a skeleton key. Someone came in with a key and unlocked the door, Ted. How long's Tim been gone?"

Beresford said slowly, "Since about two o'clock."

"Did he set a time for coming back?"

"No—but he hoped to make it before you got here." Beresford rubbed his chin slowly. "Damn it, Tim wouldn't let anyone catch up with him and steal his key!"

"If the old boy was snatched, why shouldn't Tim be? They knew he was working on the job. Pretty show, if they've got Tim, too." Dawlish laughed, but didn't sound amused.

"Going to tell Felicity about this?"

"Not yet," said Dawlish. "I'm beginning to have a lot of respect for this Mr. Rutter, if it is Mr. Rutter; or Mr. Mascatti. Know anything about a Soho club called the Golden Shoe?"

Beresford grinned.

"Home for country visitors who like to think they're seeing London night-life. I took two of Joan's cousins along there a month ago. They do it quite nicely. Lot's of dancing lovelies, dressed just enough to satisfy the police, subdued lights, plenty of exotic music, hostages of both sexes. I mean hostesses." His grin broadened. "I had a job to get the rustics home before four a.m. Odd thing, it wasn't wildly expensive, either. Why?"

"Mascatti, the owner, may be in this show."

"Second sight?" inquired Beresford, interestedly.

"We caught a brace of prisoners and they talked," said Dawlish. "The picture isn't all dark. That reminds me, we haven't finished looking in that wallet. I'll unlock these cases and Felicity can get her dresses hung." He carried the two into the bedroom, unlocked all five, and then went back into the living-room. Felicity came in, with tea for herself and a pile of sandwiches for Beresford. She was herself again. Felicity's storms seldom lasted for long.

"What's that?" she asked, as Dawlish took out the wallet.

"Left behind by old Kimble." Dawlish took out the contents of the other side of the wallet. There were several oddments, and two or three snapshots, and in another partition seven pound notes. He looked at the snapshots. One was probably Kimble with an elderly woman, perhaps his wife. The next was of a young man, an attractive-looking fellow with obvious family likeness to Kimble.

He handed these to Beresford.

"That's Kimble," Beresford said, as Dawlish studied the third. It was of a girl. She couldn't have been much more than twenty when this had been taken—and although it wasn't a particularly good snap, something about her face arrested him. It had a charm it was difficult to place.

He handed it to Beresford—and set off an explosion.

Beresford cried: "Great Scott! That's the girl who was at the station. She—"

Dawlish and Felicity stared at him, Felicity in bewilderment, Dawlish inquiringly.

CHAPTER V

THE GOLDEN SHOE

"Sorry," mumbled Beresford. Getting excited always embarrassed him. "Odd show. She was at Victoria, waiting for the train. Couldn't mistake her. Couldn't help looking at her, either, she was—"

"A pretty hussy," Felicity said tartly.

"Well, yes." Beresford took her seriously. "And no, if you see what I mean. Not really *pretty*. Attractive. Had a funny little nose and her chin was a little bit on one side, I remember. Nice eyes. She—"

"I wonder if you will explain all this to Joan," said Felicity.

Dawlish gripped her arm and squeezed; asking her not to be even tartly flippant.

"She had a nice figure," Beresford went on, and managed to make it clear that 'nice' was an understatement. "Well turned out and polished, and stamping up and down the platform as if she couldn't wait for that train to come in. I watched her—"

Felicity snorted.

"—and a queer thing happened. A smooth type came along and grinned at her. *Very* nicely turned out, in dove grey."

Beresford wrinkled his nose. "If you see what I mean. Had a pretty cool grin and made a beeline for her. She wasn't having any. Turned and hurried off, and he chased her. I went to see if they met, but they'd disappeared, and the train was due any minute."

"What was there about her that interested you?" Dawlish asked.

"Darling," said Felicity sweetly, "she was an attractive girl with a funny little nose."

"Darling," said Dawlish, "I shall shortly put your funny little nose into the kitchen, and lock the door on it. What made you so interested, Ted? The pacing up and down?"

"Rather more. She was on edge. Not just impatient. I'd say she was frightened. She was certainly waiting for someone off the train, but the smooth type stopped her. Probably why he came." Beresford looked almost ashamed of himself for advancing a theory, for he was a man of great humility. "Thing is—who was she waiting for? I mean, as she obviously knows old Kimble, he'd hardly have her picture in his pocket if she didn't. Was she waiting for you?"

Felicity said: "Oh, no. Pretty girls with snub noses always drive Pat away."

Beresford was earnest. "It wasn't exactly snub, Fel."

"Tip-tilted?"

"That's it."

Felicity groaned. "Men," she said, and poured herself out another cup of tea. She wasn't a teetotaller, but didn't drink a great deal.

Dawlish dropped into the huge armchair, stretched out his legs and picked up the tankard, which was half full of beer. He drank. He looked lazy and unimaginative, and even Felicity watched him with bewilderment; a man she could not really understand. Beresford sat on the arm of another chair as if waiting for the oracle to speak.

"It's about a hundred to one that she wanted to see me," mused Dawlish. "Did Kimble ever describe this Rutter?"

"No, and I didn't think to ask him. Sorry."

"As Trivett knows him, we can pick it up when we want to." Dawlish looked lazily across at his wife. "I've never seen you so bright-eyed, my sweet. How you'll settle down to early nights and in a double bed again, I just don't know. Wouldn't be a bad idea to break yourself in gently, would it? I mean, a halfway stage between the *Tabarin* and a country cottage. How about putting on that frontless creation—or the backless model—and coming along to the Golden Shoe? There's a man there named Mascatti."

"Want me, too?" asked Beresford, without eagerness.

"Mind holding the fort?"

"That's me," said Beresford, with relief. "I'll give Joan a ring and tell her I'll be home latish, too. Expect anything to happen here?"

"No. You might let the chap out of the cupboard in the little spare room, give him a bottle of beer and a chance to stretch his legs, and then shut him up again. Name of Percy Dipper."

"Do you mean—" began Felicity, but gave it up.

Dawlish drove out of the mews, just after ten o'clock, and headed for Victoria. It was not until they were at Hyde Park Corner that Felicity awoke to the fact that they were going away from the West End, not towards it. She was snug in a silver fur wrap and Dior's latest creation, and although she would not have admitted it, she was happy. In moods such as this, Dawlish could exasperate and anger her, but it brought out a quality which made him different from other men.

"Have you lost your bump of direction?" she asked. "We're not going to Montmartre."

"Little job to do first," said Dawlish. "I locked a chap in the garage."

Felicity nearly choked.

"Name of Percy?" she gasped.

"No. Scotty. Works for Percy."

"How do you do it?" Felicity asked helplessly. "You couldn't have had much more than an hour."

"Everything went my way," said Dawlish. "I won't be long with Scotty."

Scotty was asleep in the garage. Dawlish shook and called him; Scotty still slept. Dawlish carried him to the car and they went to the flat. Scotty's pulse and eyes seemed normal.

Half an hour later he was awake, but stupid. Twenty minutes later still, his stupor left him. He gave his name, his address and his solemn oath that he would never do anything against Mr. Dawlish again, and almost ran out of the mews in his relief. Dawlish wondered what Scotty had taken, before starting off again for Nick Mascatti's.

"I suppose," said Felicity patiently, "that you're making sure we aren't followed."

They had not gone straight to Soho, but were now near the Golden Shoe.

"Not quite," said Dawlish. "Just trying to find out who the chap is."

Felicity twisted round in her seat and stared out of the back window. The lights of several cars were behind them.

"Which one?" she asked resignedly.

"Second. Little Austin. It started off at the flat. Did a good job, took short cuts and got ahead of us two or three times. Using plenty of manpower, aren't they?"

Felicity nodded.

"Percy Dipper runs a little gang, I fancy, and probably has a dozen members and another dozen hangers-on, so manpower isn't a problem." Dawlish swung the car off the main road and pulled up at a corner, near a dozen parked cars. The Golden Shoe was just round the corner. He lit a cigarette and put his arm round Felicity's shoulder. The Austin passed and went straight on, until it was some way off, where it turned left.

"Rather go and stay with Joan for the night?"

"I would *not*. I shall probably enjoy the club," said Felicity.

Dawlish kissed her lightly on the cheek, then leaned across and opened her door.

"Let's go."

Neon lighting in the shape of a big yellow shoe hung outside the club. A commissionaire in a gold-braided uniform stood in the front of the narrow doorway. The house was one of several in a short street, and only the sign and bright yellow paint distinguished it from others. That was plenty. The commissionaire bade them a cultured good evening and led them to the reception desk. A bright-eyed, heavily made-up girl asked in sultry tones whether they were members—and made them members for the paltry sum of five shillings; guineas were more usual. They were led up a flight of narrow stairs which were covered with red carpet. The sound of music came clearly as they reached the first landing.

"You know," said Dawlish, "this isn't bad. Value for money." He waved at the paintings on the walls; a modified show of Bacchanalia.

A smooth-speaking young man with a thin line of moustache, a pale blue tuxedo and a bright mauve tie, led them into the club proper. The room was unexpectedly large, and probably spread over two houses. The dance space was in the middle; a good band was playing a zamba, and a dozen couples were dancing, on ample space; in fact there was room for fifty couples, and Dawlish doubted whether the tables accommodated more than seventy. The wall decorations were neither hideous nor too blatant.

"Corner?" asked Dawlish.

"I think I can find one vacant, sir." They were led to a corner away from the band. "I hope you'll enjoy your evening with us. I'll send a waiter."

The young exquisite nodded and smiled suavely and disappeared, leaving them with a wine list. Dawlish ran his eye down the list and decided that the prices were more reasonable than anywhere else in London.

"Too good to be true. No fleecing," he said. "Did I tell you that you look ravishing?"

"No. Pat, who do you expect to find here?"

"Percy Dipper says he is employed by Nick Mascatti and Nick runs this place. So I thought a word with Nick could be useful, even if only to hear him say he's never heard of Percy. I wonder how one gets into the presence. I—"

He broke off.

A burst of laughter came from a table near the dance floor. A man stood up unsteadily, leaned against the table with one hand and grabbed a girl by the other. Only she wasn't exactly a girl, even at twenty feet the crowsfeet at her eyes were visible. She wore a girlish white gown, her hair was hennaed and her voice was strident.

"Ducky, you can't even *stand*!" she cried.

"Shtand? Nonshensh. Look at me." The man took his hand off the table and stretched his arm out, released the woman and stretched the other out and stood as a man might on a tight rope, swaying from side to side. Suddenly he hiccoughed; but he remained standing and swaying.

"Ducky, don't—"

"Dansh," said the man. "I inshist. Dansh. Come along." He took the plump arm again and walked unsteadily towards the dance floor. He was tall and thin, and some people would have called him good-looking. He swayed violently and his companion grabbed him.

"Dearie, it's no use, you'd never—"

"*Dansh*," insisted the tall, thin man. He was well-dressed in a dinner jacket, but his dark hair, getting rather thin, was rumpled. His expression was one of great concentration; a drunkard's look. He set his lips and made for the floor. Two couples moved, to get out of his way.

"Teach you zhamba," he announced. "Thish way. Look."

He began to dance. It was as much alike a zamba as a foxtrot is like a quadrille. His partner stood a yard away from him, and he didn't touch her, just went on with his absurd gyrations, rear waggling, feet going to and fro, an expression of studied concentration on his face.

He stopped, and bowed.

"Shee? Jus' like that. Come onsh." He grabbed his partner, and she shrieked with laughter. Other couples steered clear of them. A party in the middle of the room, whose dinner-jackets and long dresses looked as if they had recently come out of storage, were staring in awed fascination at the spectacle.

The music stopped abruptly; there was a moderate outburst of clapping, and the floor cleared. The drunk didn't stop dancing; his partner's laughter was almost hysterical.

"Be sherious." His protest was audible all over the room. "Very wunnerful dansh. Sou-sou-soush American. Wunnerful dancers. Got—*rhythm*. Shee? Like this." He let his partner go and performed more weird and wonderful antics. "*I've* got rhythm. Capital R. You try. Hold me closher. Now . . ." he hugged his partner, who was showing all the outward signs of hysterical laughter but no longer making a sound.

The smooth young man who had welcomed the Dawlishes went towards the couple, and touched the drunk's arm.

"Excuse me, sir, the dancing's stopped. Will you go back to your table?"

"Eh? Wash 'at?"

"The dancing has stopped, sir."

"Stopped? Wash stopped?"

"The dancing, sir."

The thin-faced man frowned, leaned forward, rested a hand on the other's shoulder, and said solemnly:

"Hashn't, you know. I'm shtill danshing. Customer alwaysh right. Didn't anyone tell you?"

"Yes, sir, of course." The smooth man was obviously determined not to have a real scene. "There'll be more dancing shortly. If you will return to your table—"

"Don't be shilly," said the drunk, in a deep, resonant voice. "Ridiculush. Lishen, Gertie, did you hear him? Man wansh me to dance on table. Silly fellow. Can't dance on table. Old-fashioned. Li-li-licenshous, thash whash it ish. Lesh dansh!" He took her in his arms again.

"I'm sorry, sir, this is an interval. There's no music," said the young man in the tuxedo. "If you—"

"No—*mushic*?"

"That's right, sir. You can't dance without music."

The thin-faced man looked owlish, consulted the floor, consulted the ceiling, and agreed.

"Very logical. No mushic, no dansh. Very bad. Lazy sonsh of gunsh. Grave problem. No—mushic. I—" He hesitated, then his face cleared, he beamed, turned and made a rush for the orchestra platform. "Make own mushic!" he cried in triumph.

He grabbed a pair of clappers and a tambourine and began to wave and work them, keeping some kind of rhythm, and started to dance.

He also started to sing.

The little man in the tuxedo said sharply, "Either you come off the floor, sir, or I shall have to ask you to leave the club."

"Eh?"

"Either you—"

"I heard you first time. Goin' to throw me out, eh? *Me?* Not on your shilly li'l life, chappie. Not a chansh. Tell you why." He snapped the clappers under the other's nose, and grinned. "You throw me out—*I'll* throw you out. What are you going to do about it? Wanna fight?"

Felicity, watching and listening, touched Dawlish's arm and said:

"Well, Tim wasn't kidnapped, anyhow. Do you think he's really drunk, or is he fooling?"

CHAPTER VI

BRAWL

Unsmilingly, Dawlish watched Tim Jeremy squaring up to the man in the tuxedo. Two hefty men moved from the door and threaded their way between the tables, bearing down on Jeremy with obvious purpose. Jeremy appeared not to notice them, and glared aggressively into the other man's face.

"You heard me. Wanna fight?"

"I hope you will be reasonable, sir, and go quietly. I don't want any trouble."

"So you don't wan' any trouble. *I* don't mind a bit o' trouble." Jeremy giggled. "Good all-rounder, thash me. Bit o' fluff, bit o' trouble, bit o'—"

He stopped.

The large men had ranged themselves on either side of him. An elderly man stood up and shepherded two young women out. Jeremy glanced at the brawny individual on his left, then at the other on his right. Their intention had obviously dawned on him. He drew himself up with great dignity.

"Gertie," he said. "Wait for me downshtairs. Don't stay to witnesh vulgar brawl. I won't be long."

"Now, Timmy, dear—"

Timmy dear pointed majestically towards the door.

"Go, Gertie." His finger quivered, but he kept his balance. Gertie turned. One of the large men put a hand on Jeremy's arm. Jeremy stared down at it—and then appeared to be galvanized as by an exploding stick of dynamite. He smashed a straight left into one face, grabbed the other man's arm, twisted, and sent him flying across the room. The victim crashed into a table, a woman screamed, bottles and glasses fell. The first man was on his knees, a bewildered look in his eyes, as if he couldn't believe that a human fist had hit so hard. The man in the tuxedo backed away nervously.

Dawlish began to smile.

Tim Jeremy picked up the clappers, clicked them towards each of the big men with a flourish, clicked them twice in the face of the man with the tuxedo, flung them on to the platform, bowed to the room at large and made his way unsteadily towards the door. In the doorway he turned and snapped his fingers, then went out with great dignity. A second or two of silence was followed by a series of thuds and a crash.

Timothy Jeremy had fallen down the stairs.

"Pat, oughtn't you to look after him? He *is* drunk." Felicity was leaning forward anxiously. "He wouldn't have fallen down the stairs if he hadn't been. Hurry."

"He'll get himself home," said Dawlish placidly.

"If he drives like that—"

"He'll have the sense to get a cab."

"He hasn't any sense, he's blotto."

"Even blotto, he'll get a cab." Dawlish watched the two big men pick themselves up. The manager spoke to them, and they went out together; they did not look as if they were going to lick their wounds.

Dawlish stood up.

"Perhaps you're right." He hurried across the room, as the band came back and struck up a quick-step. Dawlish reached the head of the stairs and saw the gold-braided commissionaire and the painted cloak-room girl picking Tim Jeremy up. Jeremy looked silly and forlorn. The two chuckers-out were halfway down the stairs. One growled:

"Leave him alone."

"Oh, don't—" began the girl.

"Get out of the way." The two men were now at the foot of the stairs, and Jeremy stood with his back to them, his pose one of absolute dejection. They moved together. Dawlish went down the stairs as if catapulted. As the men reached Jeremy, he reached them. He grabbed the backs of their necks and cracked their heads together; the report was like a pistol shot. He flung them aside—and they couldn't have known what happened as they reeled away.

Jeremy straightened up, went forward, unsteadily, breathed deeply of the cold night air, and bellowed:

"*Taxi!*"

"Timmy, dear." Gertie appeared from her sanctuary. "You've got a car, don't—"

"*Taxi!*" roared Jeremy. "Porter, *cab!*" He almost fell on Gertie. "Doan' wonna drive. Never drive when I'm drunksh. Anyone tell you? I'm drunksh. My father always said, get blotto like a man, Timothy, but never drive yourself home. Wishe man. Like me. *Taxi!*"

Dawlish watched the taxi disappear, then went upstairs. Everything was normal, except that the elderly man and the two girls weren't at their table. Felicity was looking towards the door, and Dawlish grinned and waved. He reached the table.

"Dance?"

She stood up. "What happened?"

"He's drunk."

"I told you that, but what makes you sure he isn't fooling?"

"He called a cab—and if he weren't drunk, he'd prefer the car. He told Gertie about the time-honoured advice his father gave to all who were over the eight." Dawlish swung Felicity into the quick-step, and people began to look at them, for Dawlish was nearly a head taller than anyone else in the room, and they danced together superbly. "We'll worry about how and why he did it afterwards. Just now we want a chat with Mascatti." Dawlish's gaze roamed the room, and he saw a man come in and stand by the door, looking round.

He would have been noticeable anywhere. He wasn't big, not even tall, but was perfectly dressed in a dinner jacket, and had a figure which looked as if it had been made for his clothes. He had a fine head, his black hair was going grey at the sides, giving a touch of distinction. The hair was rather long, but well-kept and brushed straight back from his high forehead.

Dawlish doubted whether he had ever seen a more handsome man. It was as if a new star had stepped out of Hollywood. It was in his manner as well as his looks; he was in superb control of himself.

"See him?" Dawlish asked.

Felicity was staring towards the door.

"I see you have," Dawlish said dryly. "The perfect man. Could it be Mascatti?"

Felicity said: "Surely . . ." and her voice trailed off. She laughed, as Dawlish whirled her round. "All right, darling, I won't stare again."

"Then you'll be the only woman in the room who doesn't."

Felicity stared. . . .

The handsome man went to two occupied tables, talked for a few minutes, then went to others, further away. The music stopped. Dawlish went the long way round to his table, and heard a man say:

"Yes, Mr. Mascatti, wonderful, thanks."

"I'm sorry about that incident," said Mascatti. He had a deep, pleasant voice with an accent slight enough to be fascinating. At closer quarters his eyes showed curiously light brown.

"Oh, that was nothing. Just a drunk."

"We try to avoid unpleasantness," said Mascatti. He moved on to another table; apparently it was his custom to speak to each guest. He was a long time approaching Dawlish, so long that Dawlish wondered if he were being deliberately avoided.

They danced a foxtrot.

The music stopped. Dawlish led a laughing Felicity back to the table. Mascatti appeared not to notice them, Dawlish ordered another Pimms for himself, and lit a cigarette—and Mascatti appeared at his side as the Pimms arrived.

"Good evening, Mr. Dawlish."

Dawlish looked up brightly. "Why, hallo!"

"I hope you're enjoying your evening here."

"Not bad," said Dawlish. "Not bad at all. Thanks."

"I'm glad to hear it. I am Mascatti." He smiled; but his eyes weren't smiling.

"Well, well," said Dawlish. "The great man himself. Nice of you. Yes, everything's fine, even the unrehearsed cabaret. When does the professional one come on?"

"At twelve-thirty," said Mascatti, and looked at Felicity with obvious admiration.

"Goody," said Dawlish inanely. "Oh—meet my wife. *Mrs. Dawlish.*"

"I'm happy to meet you, Mrs. Dawlish. I'm afraid you will

find this very dull after Paris, but we do our best." Mascatti managed to make everything he said sound impressive. "I hope you will persuade your husband to come again, we are always glad to entertain personalities."

Felicity smiled. "Thank you."

"Personalities?" echoed Dawlish. "You can't mean me. Good lord!" He hugged Felicity. "Hear that—he thinks I'm a personality."

Mascatti looked faintly disgusted.

"I hope you enjoy the rest of the evening," he said, and bowed and went on. Dawlish watched him, and then sipped his drink. It tasted all right. He sipped again—and then his smile became more fatuous than ever.

"Can he be a *rogue*?" Felicity asked.

"Sweetness, he can be," said Dawlish. "Someone's doctored my drink. High-powered alcoholic content, one of these would make me rolling drunk. As drunk as Tim. See the joke?"

"But—"

"What's more, I'm going to get drunk," said Dawlish. "Or so he'll think. I'll pour most of the stuff in your glass—no, better, we'll change." With swiftness of hand that almost deceived Felicity, he put a glass to his lips, pretended to drink, then placed it in front of him. It was Felicity's, and nearly empty. That in front of Felicity was now nearly full. "Going to see it through?" he asked.

Felicity said, "I'm not sure you're right."

"You can be sure. On the whole, I think you'd better go. Try and get me out when I start showing tipsy, and when I won't come, shoot off by yourself. Drive to the nearest 'phone and ring the flat, ask Ted to come here, and wait outside. If I don't show up within an hour, Ted had better come in."

"I suppose I'd better," Felicity said reluctantly.

* * *

Twenty minutes later Dawlish sat alone at his table, drinking and smoking. He didn't go gay, like Tim, but morose. He slouched in his chair, hiccoughed loudly, and kept calling for his glass to be refilled. None of the later drinks was doctored. He narrowed his eyes and made them look bleary, and he appeared not to notice that several people, including the two strong-arm men, were watching him closely. Half an hour after Felicity had left the tuxedo-clad manager came over to him.

Dawlish looked up, blankly.

"I wonder if you would spare me a few minutes, Mr. Dawlish."

"Eh?"

"Come with me for a few minutes, sir. Mr. Mascatti would very much like a word with you."

Dawlish tried to get up, and collapsed. The strong-arm men came forward and helped; they had a job to hold him, for he leaned all of his great weight on them.

"This way, sir," said the manager, and Dawlish staggered after him, watched by everyone in the room.

CHAPTER VII

MASCATTI

Mascatti sat at a large desk in a large room on the floor above the dance-room. It was sound-proof; no whisper of music reached it. It was luxurious without being opulent; walnut-panelled walls, modern furniture, a thick-piled carpet, some water colours on the walls which would have held a place of honour in any exhibition. This background suited Mascatti perfectly; he seemed part of the room.

The strong-arm men went out; only the exquisite remained with them.

"Want me?" Dawlish hiccoughed.

"It's good of you to come," said Mascatti. "Mr. Dawlish, you are the second man who has got drunk here tonight, and I know that the first is a friend of yours. Mr. Jeremy."

Dawlish gulped. "Supposing he is?"

"I just want to find out why," Mascatti said. "What good do you expect to do?"

"Right wrongs," declared Dawlish. "*You* ask questions. What a nerve. *I'll* ask 'em. Why send Percy Dipper after me? Eh? Answer me that."

Mascatti showed a reaction, but not quite what Dawlish expected. Surprise gave way to disgust.

"I don't know why Dipper told you that," said Mascatti, "But he lied. He has lied to others, about me. Did he really say that?"

Dawlish hiccoughed, and growled:

"He did. What have you done with Kimble? Where is he? What have you done with him?"

Mascatti's eyes cleared, as if one puzzle was solved. He might be a rogue but he was certainly no fool. He pondered for a few seconds, then leaned forward, with his hands clasped on the desk.

"Kimble and I have had a great deal of business together in the past few years, and we don't always see eye-to-eye, but I have no idea where he is—I had no idea that he was missing. Did Dipper say that I had?"

Dawlish muttered, "Two and two make four."

"I know that Kimble has been hostile, of late, but I didn't expect that he would use Dipper to blackguard me—if that has happened, I confess, I don't know what has happened, but I have nothing to hide from you. When did Kimble first get in touch with you? Have you seen him?"

"Forget it."

"I wish you would tell me what you've been told," said Mascatti. "Perhaps you will, if I am frank with you. Kimble stole something from me, Mr. Dawlish. He doesn't want me to get it back, and by pretending that it's his own property he could have grounds for appealing to you for help. If his story were true, of course, he would go to the police. He can't go to them because they might find out that he isn't quite what he's supposed to be. Surely any man who used Dipper as an envoy is suspect. But"—Mascatti shrugged—"I am guessing, of course. When *did* he first get in touch with you? Was it through Dipper?"

Dawlish screwed up his eyes, as if in an effort to remember, and then muttered:

"Not sure. Wasn't interested."

"I'm glad to hear it. What made you interested?"

"Not really interested now," rumbled Dawlish. "Kimble can pull out his own chestnuts. Plenty of mine own. Leave detection to detectives. That kind of thing. Like a spot of excitement, and I *won't* be followed about." He sounded peevish. "Understand? Chappie followed me from the station, had to do something about it. Told me Percy Dipper put him up to it, saw Percy. *He* named you."

"I'm not surprised," said Mascatti, but looked puzzled. "But where does Kimble come in? I was told that he had tried to interest you, and am anxious to find out if you are going to help him."

Dawlish grunted.

"I think I can see what has happened. Kimble came to see you and blackguarded me. Later, Dipper attacked you, and named me as his employer. He's done that before. He once worked for me, and I had to dismiss him—he has been venomous ever since. Somehow I have to convince you that they lied to you, hoping to prejudice you against me."

"Why should they?" demanded Dawlish.

"Since they were presenting me as a villain, what better?" Mascatti smiled, as if suddenly amused. "You are not working for Kimble, if I understand you."

"Certainly not."

Mascatti laughed.

"Then will you help me?"

Dawlish gasped.

"*You* need help?"

"Since I am being made out to be a rogue, I need to protect

myself. I suppose Kimble said that some documents had been stolen from him?"

Dawlish drank.

"Don't know," he said decidedly. "Wasn't interested. Wouldn't have done a thing if I hadn't been followed. Dipper named you, not Kimble. Never like being followed." He screwed up his eyes. "What *did* he say? I—oh, yes, bleated about blackmail. As if I cared. No money in it for me. Not *real* money. Thinks I'm a Robin Hood." Dawlish leered. "Got more sense."

"So he talked of blackmail?"

"Very mysterious about it all," declared Dawlish. "Wouldn't tell me anything. Told him I wouldn't touch the case. My wife wouldn't let me, anyhow. She's tired of the way I go about doing work the police ought to do." He was virtuously indignant.

Mascatti smiled urbanely.

"A beautiful woman with common sense is a rarity, Mr. Dawlish, you're a lucky man. Your friends—"

"Friends!" snorted Dawlish. "Jeremy and Beresford? Tongue-twisters for you. Couple of reckless idiots. Always telling them so. I took my wife away, Kimble couldn't follow us to Paris. Well, anyway he didn't. So he went after them. Told them the old story, and they wanted me to do something. Soon fixed them. I—Good Lord!"

He sat up, eyes rounded with amazement.

Mascatti waited.

"The addle-pated son of a gun," roared Dawlish. "He tried to handle it himself. Tim, I mean. And got drunk!" He bellowed with laughter. "Always gets into trouble if he tries to do a job himself. Hasn't got the gift. Different with me," he went on earnestly. "Can't help it if I've a gift, can I?"

"You've used it brilliantly."

"That's right," said Dawlish. "Brilliantly. That's me." He patted his chest, hiccoughed, had another drink and fumbled for his cigarettes. A gold box of them was pushed towards him, and the exquisite appeared at his side with a lighted match. "Ta." He made three attempts to light the cigarette and nearly blew the match out. "Ah. That's the trouble with Tim. No sense. Fancy getting *drunk*."

"He certainly made a fool of himself."

"Told him so," declared Dawlish. "Said it to his face. 'No job for us,' I said. 'Keep off.' He wouldn't listen. Had Ted waiting for me at the station, didn't give me a minute's peace. You ought to have heard my wife tearing a strip off him." He grinned, sneeringly. "Then this chap started following me about and got my goat. I—"

He stopped, and stared.

Mascatti smiled. Dawlish drew himself up, started to get to his feet, and dropped into his chair again heavily. He leaned forward.

"You're *Mascatti*," he announced aggressively.

"Yes, Mr. Dawlish, and—"

"My turn. Let me get a word in." Dawlish waggled a big forefinger. "You're Mascatti. Put Percy Dipper on to me. I want to talk to you." He hitched the chair nearer the table. "Don't do it again. I won't have it. That's why I came here. To tell you—keep off. When I'm roused," said Dawlish with great solemnity. "I'm dangerous. Understand? I'm a dangerous man to annoy."

"I'm quite sure you are," Mascatti said mildly. "I would rather have you on my side. If Kimble should worry you again, will you tell me about it, and let me know exactly what slander he is spreading?"

"You want me to report to you?"

"Yes. I would like your help, in any case, to find out whether Kimble is behind Dipper's venomous attitude." Mascatti spread out his hands. "It is not a matter I would care to handle through the police, I would much prefer to find out quietly."

Dawlish collapsed into his chair, shook his head, scowled, and sipped his drink. Then he consulted the ceiling.

"Not worth my while," he said firmly.

Mascatti said softly: "Perhaps I could make it worth your while, Mr. Dawlish. I'm not a mean man. Of course, if you're going to talk in really big figures I can't meet you, but if it's reasonable—" He broke off.

"What do you call reasonable?"

"Well . . ." Dawlish deliberated, shrugged, grumbled to himself, and then fixed Mascatti firmly with his gaze.

"Two hundred pounds," he said abruptly.

"For what?"

"Letting you know what Kimble says."

"How many times?"

Dawlish frowned and considered, and then wagged his finger again.

"Don't get smart. A month. Suit you?"

Mascatti said gently: "Yes, Mr. Dawlish, I think that's very fair. You will receive two hundred pounds each month while the need continues, for passing on to me anything that Kimble tells you. From that, I should be able to learn all I need to know. And the first payment should be in advance, of course. Do you mind one-pound notes?"

Dawlish gaped.

Mascatti chuckled. "I'm a business man, Mr. Dawlish, and I don't see why we shouldn't conclude our deal quickly. I'll have Rutter get the money out of the safe. It won't take five minutes. Rutter . . ." He looked up at the exquisite.

"I'll get it right away, Mr. Mascatti."

Mascatti nodded, and Rutter went out. Dawlish didn't watch

him go. So this was Rutter, and Mascatti didn't hesitate to name him. It was all so smooth. He watched Mascatti pour him out another whisky-and-soda. He wasn't sure that Mascatti believed him to be drunk. He wasn't at all sure of anything—unless Mascatti wanted to make sure Kimble didn't get his help.

Dawlish stopped thinking.

Another door opened, but Rutter didn't come in. A girl did.

She looked young, in face and figure she had everything. She carried a note-book and pencil in her hand.

"I'm sorry, Mr. Mascatti, I didn't know you were engaged. You told me to come at this time." Her English was good but she had a slight accent. Dawlish didn't recognize the accent but he did recognize her as the girl of the photograph and Victoria Station.

CHAPTER VIII

FREE GIFT

"It's all right, Carlotta." Mascatti smiled. "I'd forgotten you were coming just now. I'll ring for you later."

She apologized again, and went out. Dawlish had an odd impression that she disliked him on sight. Imagination? It had shown in the look in her eyes; a look very near contempt. That took the edge off his surprise at recognizing her.

"I say," he boomed. "What a charmer. You sly old dog. Secretary?"

Mascatti said smoothly, "Yes, one of mine—a young girl whom I am helping." The preciseness of his phrasing was odd. "So you admire beauty?"

"My dear chap! I'm human, aren't I? I could go places with a charmer like that. If you know what I mean." He dropped into a chair and groped for his glass. Rutter came in, carrying a wad of notes. Rutter had a toothy smile; he would have looked well in dove grey and he measured up to Beresford's description of the man at Victoria Station.

"Shall I count it, Mr. Mascatti?"

"Yes, of course, Mr. Dawlish—"

"Forget it," said Dawlish. "I know honest men when I see them. More likely to be two hundred and one than one ninety-nine." He hiccoughed. "Say nine-ninety-nine! Doctor's orders. Er—think your secretary has any free time?"

"I have no idea," said Mascatti.

Dawlish winked at Rutter, took the wad of notes, stood up, stepped carefully from the desk towards the door Rutter had used. Mascatti reached it first, opened it with a bow, and waited as Dawlish went through.

"Goo' night."

"Good night, Mr. Dawlish."

Rutter followed Dawlish to the front door downstairs and watched him drive off; he clashed his gears twice. Felicity and Beresford, nearby in Beresford's car, followed him.

At half past one that morning Carlotta Morlay opened the door of her two-roomed flatlet in Westminster, and started when she saw a man rise from the settee. She wasn't alarmed, just surprised. The man had an eager expression and a hint of naïveté which stamped him as very young. He had wavy fair hair and a good skin, was fresh-looking, but not handsome.

"You're late, aren't you?" He was abrupt.

"I'm often late," said Carlotta. She took off a small hat and flung it into a chair, poked her fingers through her mass of dark hair, and dropped on to the sofa. "You oughtn't to be here at this hour, Terry."

"Who cares?" He leaned towards her. "How did things go? Did you see Dawlish?"

"Don't mention *that* brute to me!"

"Brute? Dawlish? Now, listen, Dawlish is—"

"Dawlish is a drunken, lecherous brute. If I'd known what I do now, I wouldn't have suggested that your father should go to him. It—it's folly. He actually took a bribe, to *spy* on your father."

Terence Kimble gasped, "No!"

"Oh, go home," said Carlotta. "You make me more and more tired. You're such a young fool. Fools run in your family, your father—"

"Now, look here," protested Terry in a quieter voice which gave him a touch of maturity. "You're tired and overwrought. Are you sure about this or are you dreaming?"

"I was there when he took this bribe. That is, when he agreed to take it. I was going to see if I was wanted any more. He was with Mascatti. There is no hope for your father if Dawlish is the best man you can find."

Terry said slowly: "I don't understand. I've always believed that Dawlish was an absolute winner."

"Well, he is not. Terry, go home, please. I have a severe headache and I am ill with disappointment. Has Dawlish asked your father for money?"

"But Father hasn't seen him yet!"

"Do not you deceive yourself," said Carlotta.

"He hasn't, I tell you."

Obviously she didn't believe that, but she did nothing to encourage an argument.

"All right, Terry. Go home, now. I am so tired."

Terry said slowly: "Yes, I can see you are. Sorry, old girl. I should never have asked you to take that damned job. My fault. Why don't you throw it up?"

Carlotta looked at him levelly.

"Isn't that like you? Start a thing and if it gets difficult, give it up before you have really tried. And your father—oh, it doesn't matter. Go away, Terry."

He went immediately, and they hardly said good night. She

started to undress at once and was soon in bed, but it was a long time before she went to sleep. It didn't greatly matter, for she did not have to be at the office until two o'clock in the afternoon; there were consolations in everything. She sneered at herself for the thought.

It was broad daylight when she woke; and warm. She had too many bedclothes on, flung a blanket back, and sat up against her pillows. She looked round the room. It was small and shabby but at least it was clean. A few oddments of her own and some personal touches saved it from being like thousands of other small flats in London, tenanted by single girls. The pink roses in a low vase on a bamboo table were drooping; June was flaming too much for them. There was a large window with china pieces of her own, once her mothers, on the wide ledge; a French poodle, an Italian gondolier, a piece of Dresden—pieces she remembered from her childhood and had salvaged from the wreckage of a home and a family. Whenever she thought of the past, it hurt so much that she rebelled. The future had a chilling bleakness.

She got up and put on the kettle, brushed her teeth and drew the curtains in the small room where Terence Kimble had been waiting for her. Here, on the walls, were two water colours—more salvage—on the floor a square of fading carpet. Three easy chairs and two small tables were the only furniture; that gave the room an illusion of spaciousness.

She thought of Dawlish.

She hated the thought of Dawlish.

There were moments when, with the cruel clear vision of youth, she knew that the odds were too heavy against her. She was fighting in the dark and she hardly knew what she was fighting. She had always been fighting and always in the dark. Sometimes, light ahead beckoned; now there was only fog.

She was having breakfast of toast and marmalade and coffee when the front-door bell rang.

Terry Kimble? She didn't think she could face him and she knew of no one else who was likely to come so early. She set her lips as she went to the door, prepared to tell Terry she wasn't coming out.

A small lad with scrubbed face and bright eyes beamed at her, and saluted.

"'Morning, miss. Miss Morlay?"

"Yes."

"Parcel for you, miss. Sign, please." He held out a packet wrapped in brown paper and a small book. She signed in pencil, and the boy saluted again as he hurried off. She frowned at the packet. Terry wouldn't send a present by messenger, it would be too subtle for him. Terry was nice, fresh, honest and boyish, and hadn't a subtle idea in his head. Or else he was a rogue. A few weeks ago she had even thought of marrying him, she had been so desperate. Now she had seen how badly he behaved in a crisis. He was beginning to realize that marriage was out.

The packet was fastened with gummed tape; she had to get a knife to prise it up, and it took a lot of opening. Her curiosity lost itself in irritation, but the brown paper came loose at last. She opened it out—and stared at a bundle of one-pound notes.

She caught her breath.

On top of the notes was an envelope, and on this was printed: £200.

She ripped open the envelope and took out the single sheet of folded notepaper. The writing was in a clear, bold hand:

Give this to any charity you like. Be at Piccadilly Circus Station this morning as soon after eleven as you can. A man or woman will give you a white flower. Follow him—or her. Don't speak, don't show any

sign of recognition, just follow. Burn this. Say nothing to anyone.
Think more kindly of Patrick Dawlish.

She read it twice, picked up the bundle, and laughed; the laugh was so high-pitched that it was almost hysterical. She tossed the packet into the air, caught it, flung it into a chair and saw the notes break from the rubber band which held them together; there was a storm of one-pound notes. She swung round and raced into the bathroom. It was after ten already, she hadn't much time.

At twenty minutes to eleven she was ready. Dressed in a suit for out of doors, her clothes showed signs of shabbiness or shortage of money. She looked at the litter of pound notes, began to tidy them—and the front-door bell rang again.

Her heart thumped. This would certainly be Terry, and she couldn't trust Terry with news like this. She grabbed all the notes and slipped them into the drawer of the table, then hurried to the front door, wondering how she could make sure that he didn't come with her. If necessary, she would have to force a quarrel. She opened the door.

It was Rutter.

He was dressed in his dove grey and wearing a red and white spotted bow tie. He smiled as he took off his grey Homburg hat. His skin was sallow, but his complexion was good, and the little line of moustache stretched as his lips moved.

"Hallo, Carlotta. Going places?"

She hoped that she didn't show the fear she felt—he always frightened her. She wasn't sure why.

"Yes, Mr. Rutter, I am going out."

"That's fine! We'll go together."

"I am sorry, but—"

"We'll go together," said Rutter, "after we've had a little talk." He took her right wrist and held it firmly and pushed her back into the room. He kicked the door to, then let her go. Her cheeks flushed, she was raging with anger, but something about his expression stopped her from flying at him. He had narrow, dark brown eyes, and she didn't trust them.

"You and I have to reach an understanding," he said. "Sit down, honey."

She went to a chair and dropped into it.

"And when we reach an understanding I don't want any one to break it," Rutter said. "You were spying on Mascatti last night, I saw you at the door, listening. If Mascatti knew that, you wouldn't have a job. You've always told me that your job was important."

She said huskily, "It is, very important."

"You're going the right way to lose it. Mascatti hasn't any time for spies."

She was spying on Mascatti, for she believed he was making hell for Kimble—the one man in England she owed anything. Did Rutter know? Or was he snatching the chance to get some kind of hold over her?

She didn't know; she only knew he frightened her.

"There's another thing. You're too friendly with the Kimble kid; you can say good-bye to him. You want to choose your friends better. Shake young Kimble off, and I won't tell Mascatti you were listening. Get me?"

She moistened her lips.

"I'll say you get me." Rutter smiled more broadly. "You're a nice kid, Carlotta. Once you start seeing things the right way, you'll go places. Mascatti could make a fortune for you, all you want is to get on the right side of him. Now I can fix it. Just be friendly, and I can fix it—with me on your side, you can go places. Understand, honey?"

She understood only too well.

CHAPTER IX

A WHITE FLOWER

Once at Piccadilly Station, Carlotta wondered whether she should stand in the same place, or walk round slowly. People were moving about aimlessly, others hurrying from the ticket machines towards the elevators, still more looking in the shop windows or standing near the bookstalls. She watched for anyone whom she recognized, and saw no one. She began to walk, slowly, and had been at the station for ten minutes when a stocky, well-dressed man bumped into her.

"Sorry." He smiled—and thrust a white carnation into her hand. Then he passed on. She glanced down and saw the flower, had the wit not to look round immediately, held the flower lightly, and then turned slowly. The stocky man was twenty yards away looking at some books. She walked towards him, and he moved off. Soon they were in Shaftesbury Avenue. He turned into a side street of dingy shops and barrows; Soho. Not far along, there was a closed car and he got in. She noticed that he leaned back, opened the door behind him, and as she drew level, said:

"Hop in."

"Thank you."

"Read that newspaper."

There was one on the seat; she picked it up and buried her face in it, guessing what he wanted. She was amazed at these precautions. She didn't notice where they were going for the first few minutes, then saw that they were in Oxford Street. She knew that Dawlish sometimes stayed at a flat near here. The driver turned up the Edgware Road, away from Mayfair, took several side turnings, and finally stopped outside a modest little house in a modest little street. He turned and grinned at her.

"All clear."

"Are you from Dawlish?"

"Oh, yes," he said. "Pat's up to his tricks again. He didn't want anyone to know you were going to see him. This is how he works it."

"He seems to be very thorough."

"Oh, he's thorough." The young man laughed. She hadn't realized that he was young, until then. He had a bronzed face, grey eyes and a look of the open air. He wasn't quite the typical Englishman but there was something unmistakably English about him. "That's the house." He pointed.

She turned, and the door of the house opened before she reached it. Dawlish nearly filled the doorway.

"Hallo, Miss Morlay. All clear, Roger?"

"Aye, aye, sir."

"Go away and join the Navy," said Dawlish. His hand closed over Carlotta's, and he drew her smilingly into the house. "Upstairs. This place belongs to a friend of mine, a doctor. Duty calls him to this district." She smelt the faint smell of antiseptics and caught sight of a waiting-room and of another room with a long bench in it and a tray of instruments. The stairs were narrow, and Dawlish followed her up. They went into a room at the back of the house. She hadn't realized how tall and massive Dawlish was.

"Sit down and make yourself at home," he said, and offered cigarettes.

"Thank you."

"What did Rutter want?" he asked.

The fact that he knew Rutter had been to see her startled her, and she showed it. Dawlish chuckled, and the laughter put her at her ease. She said:

"He knew I listened to you and Mascatti at the door last night, and came to tell me."

"Oh," said Dawlish, and read much into her silence. "Not a nice chap."

"How did you know he'd been to see me?"

"My spies," he said expansively. "We thought it wise to watch the place, I didn't want you to disappear, too."

Her mood changed in a flash.

"Who else has disappeared?"

Dawlish looked at her thoughtfully; almost doubtfully. She felt a rush of disquiet, but didn't speak. He drew deeply on his cigarette, and dropped into a large armchair—large enough for him to sit in with comfort.

"Don't you know?"

"No."

"Didn't Terry Kimble come to see you last night?"

"Well, yes, he did, but—"

"Didn't he say anything?"

"Not about a disappearance. Who?"

Dawlish said slowly, "His father."

"Oh, *no!*" she cried.

Dawlish watched her fighting against distress, and seemed to approve.

"Are you sure?" She spoke slowly. "When did it happen?"

"Last night. He was waiting to see me, at the flat of a friend of mine. He was taken away."

"Was he—hurt?"

"I shouldn't think so," said Dawlish. "Would you expect him to be?"

"I—I hardly know," she said. "I only know that he has been frightened for a long time. Haven't you seen him?"

"Not yet."

"You told Mascatti—"

Dawlish grinned. "I wanted to pull the wool over Mascatti's eyes, and I think a little stuck. Partly, anyhow. He thought I was drunk and he now thinks I'm in his pay. No reason why he shouldn't go on thinking so. How long have you worked for Mascatti?"

"For about three months."

"What's he like to work for?"

"I have to admit that he's very good. I—I quite like him. He's always friendly and polite and never—unpleasant, like Rutter."

"I can believe Rutter is," said Dawlish. "I don't quite get the set-up. Whom did you meet first? Mascatti or Kimble?"

"Oh, Kimble," she said quickly. "I have known him for years. You see . . ."

She began to talk; and as she talked, realized that she hadn't felt like telling the story for many years. There was something about the giant who sat with his legs stretched out, looking completely relaxed, which had a soothing and yet stimulating effect.

It was really the story of her life.

She was the daughter of an English doctor who had spent most of his life in Czechoslovakia, and a Czech woman. Almost from her earliest days she could remember trouble and anxiety, because of Germany. Kimble had often sent patients to her father. Kimble had offered to get the family out of the country after Munich; her father had refused to go. Politically they had been to the left, so her father had good reason to fear the Nazis.

He had been among the first they had taken away.

She had never seen him again.

With her mother, she had lived through the occupation, and been 'freed' by the Russians. They had lived uneasily for a year or two, and planned to come to England. Kimble was their only contact—and when they had wanted to come, he had been in America. They had started out; her mother had been taken ill and died before leaving the country.

The Communist *coup d' état* overwhelmed the Government.

Carlotta had been left entirely on her own. No friends; no relatives; and a member of a family now politically 'unsafe'. She had escaped; she said very little about that, too. She had been in England for four months.

"I feel better for having talked to you," she said with a frankness which just missed being naïve. "You see how it was, I know. Dr. Kimble—I can't get used to his title—had often visited my father. I knew him well as a child. In letters to my mother and in messages, he was so friendly and eager to help. My mother even sent some household things, little things she valued, to him. I have them. And clothes—her own clothes. I wear them now, with little alteration. She had been sure there would be a warm welcome, but—Dr. Kimble wasn't the man I remembered. The welcome was warm enough, but empty; there was something else on his mind. I knew his look. I knew what fear is, Mr. Dawlish."

She brought fear into the room.

Dawlish said quietly: "Yes, I can guess. And he was frightened?"

"Very frightened. He couldn't think of one thing at a time for long. He was always looking over his shoulder. A dear old man, but—living in terror. He said he was sorry but he couldn't ask me to stay at his house. It was because he didn't think it was safe, although he didn't say so. I had nowhere to go—very little money, no work. He seemed to have forgotten all that. Then his son, Terry, told me that the doctor was worried about a man named Rutter, who worked for a Mr. Mascatti. Mascatti at the Golden Shoe. I went to Mascatti and asked for work—partly because I needed a job, partly because I might be able to find out what was worrying Dr. Kimble."

"Ah," said Dawlish, and leaned forward. "Have you found out?"

CHAPTER X

SHOCK FOR DAWLISH

Carlotta stood up and began to move about the room, looking at Dawlish all the time. She showed the lovely lines of her figure and the graces of her movements. She was small, but not tiny. She had beauty, of a kind—and her face compelled interest. It was not only because of her vitality; it was the mark of bitter experiences. She had learned to look in all directions at once, and she had forgotten how to rest. That made quicksilver of her.

"No. I know that there's a quarrel between Mascatti and Dr. Kimble, that Rutter seems just an employee of Mascatti, but—that's all. Mascatti pays me well—*I* think it's good, anyhow. Nine pounds a week."

"Not bad," conceded Dawlish.

"I don't like the hours very much, they're so late, but it makes little difference. Rutter made passes at me, but I wasn't very worried. I've met Rutters before."

"Yes," murmured Dawlish. "Where does Kimble's son come in? Terry, isn't it?"

"He told me his father was being blackmailed, he suspected

Rutter. I've already told you, haven't I? I've been able to find out very little, but was anxious to help Dr. Kimble. He was becoming more and more frightened. Then he decided to see you. I'd read about you and was delighted. I heard Rutter telling someone on the telephone you were arriving on that train. I had some time off, so I came to see you, because the doctor did not think you would try to help him, and I wanted to persuade you. Rutter followed me—as he's often done. He—he frightens me. I ran away."

Dawlish nodded.

"You know the rest," said Carlotta abruptly. "Except Dr. Kimble is missing. You don't know where he is."

"We'll find him," Dawlish said. "Did he tell you anything about his worries?"

"Not a word! But when I learned of them, I could understand why he didn't try to help more."

"What exactly did Terry say?"

"Only that his father is frightened, and Rutter is the cause of it. Apparently Rutter visited the doctor several times. Terry says he knows nothing of the cause of the trouble, his father has never told him."

"I'll have to meet Terry," said Dawlish. "And is that everything?"

"Yes. Mr. Dawlish, what do you think I should do to help Dr. Kimble?"

"Stay with Mascatti."

"If Rutter should tell him about my eavesdropping—"

"Try to humour Rutter," Dawlish said gently.

"I will. What—what else can I do?"

"Try to stop Rutter from telling him."

"I can for a while," said Carlotta. "Then Rutter will get too—demanding." Her smile had all the coquetry of the continental, and Dawlish chuckled. "There's no need to pretend with you," said Carlotta. "I'll stay with Mascatti while I can."

Dawlish said, "It might be dangerous."

"I'm used to danger."

"That's settled, then," said Dawlish.

"What else am I to do?"

"Nothing, yet—except what Mascatti tells you. I'll send word when I want something. Meanwhile, just keep your eyes and ears open. That's all, Carlotta! Roger Brent will drive you back and drop you near your flat."

"Is Roger Brent the man who brought me here?"

"Yes. Do anything he says, it's quite safe."

She said, "Yes, I can believe that!" There was a smile in her eyes as they shook hands.

Dawlish saw her to the front door. Brent, who was waiting in the car, jumped out eagerly.

Dawlish drove to Tim's flat, whistled as he went to the steps, whistled as he let himself in, and called, "Fel!" There was no answer, and Felicity would have heard him had she been in. He looked in every room, leaving the one where Percy Dipper was imprisoned, until last. He opened that door—and stared.

Dipper was asleep—as Scotty had been asleep. Dawlish shook him, and he stirred. He looked dazed, and in no shape to talk. Dawlish supported him across the flat, and down the steps. No one was about.

There was a small room beside the garage, and Dawlish took him there, puzzled because nothing had stirred the man out of his dazed state. Dawlish questioned him, and received sluggish answers. Dipper had been fed, there was no apparent explanation, unless he were foxing.

Dawlish locked him in and went back to the flat.

There was no sign of Felicity, no note; and she had said that she would stay in all the morning.

Dawlish went into the living-room. Tim, who had recovered quickly, had been detailed to look into Mr. Rutter's past. Ted Beresford was at his home; he had telephoned twice, hoping for action.

Dawlish felt flat and anxious. He didn't like it when Felicity was missing. Missing? It was too strong a word, but the case held a curious menace.

So much was placid, on the surface; beneath, it was boiling. Dawlish could only see the surface, and consequently felt flat.

Carlotta's story had been an anti-climax; and had rung true.

Had it been true? Or just part of the truth? Or wholly false?

He had an uncomfortable feeling that Mascatti was laughing at him.

He telephoned Scotland Yard, but Superintendent Trivett was out. A talk with Bill Trivett was one of the first things he wanted: Trivett might be able to tell him a lot about Mascatti, and perhaps more about Rutter.

Dawlish picked up a newspaper; he had seen few in the past two weeks, English papers didn't seem the same in Paris. A single column headline caught his eye:

SLEEPING DEATH AGAIN

He read of a man who had been found, apparently asleep, in a railway carriage—but was dead. Several similar deaths had been reported. The authorities, said the *Echo*, were worried.

Dawlish thought of Scotty, sleeping; and of Percy Dipper, too.

A car drew up in the mews.

He went to the window hoping to see Felicity. He saw Tim Jeremy, on his own. Tim Jeremy slammed the door of his car, a

Riley, pocketing the keys as he walked to the steps. He looked tired and droopy. Dawlish didn't open the door for him, and Tim stared when he came into the living-room and saw his friend.

He frowned. "Having a rest?"

"When you need one more," said Dawlish.

"That's right," said Jeremy. His eyes were bloodshot and his thin face looked drawn. "What a head!"

"Don't tell me you got tipsy on beer."

"I don't want any cracks out of you," growled Jeremy. "Fel tell you what happened?"

"She isn't here," said Dawlish.

Jeremy stared—frowned—and then went out. Dawlish heard him opening the door. His own feeling of disquiet increased. Jeremy came back, his frown now a scowl.

"She said she wouldn't go out."

"So she told me."

"I asked her to stay in the living-room, and look out of the window if anyone came, and not to open the door if it was someone she didn't recognize. But the beggars stole my key last night. I'd another, but one's loose."

Dawlish felt suffocated.

"Why the precautions?"

"Don't ask me. Just feel this is a devil's brew of a case," said Tim. He stood staring out of the window. "It's got under my skin. I suppose Fel nipped out to the shops. How long have you been here?"

"Half an hour."

"Then she should be back." Tim went closer to the window, so that he could see along the road leading to the mews. "Sorry about last night. I was after Rutter. Old Kimble named him. Thought I had fooled him. He went out to Putney, stayed at a pub for half an hour, and came back. Own car. Lunch time yesterday, that was. I didn't get lunch until after three, at a cafe, opposite his flat."

"Rutter's?"

"Yes. In Shepherd's Market. He didn't come out again until after five-thirty, and went straight to a pub. I followed him and had a whisky-and-soda. Stuff must have been doped." He turned, and grimaced. "Gertie was there. Remember Gertie? She helped me home—her flat, not mine. If you can call it a flat. I was as nearly blind as I've ever been, and she gave me plenty more drink. Her idea that we should go to the Golden Shoe, too."

Dawlish said softly, "I *see.*"

"I've been looking for Gertie's place this morning, but haven't found it," Tim said. "I think Gertie's deep in this."

"Probably," agreed Dawlish.

"They only thing they took was my key. Nothing else. I'll have that lock changed today, ought to have thought of it before."

"Don't," said Dawlish.

"Meaning?"

"We might turn it into a spider's parlour." Dawlish stood up and glanced out of the window and wished he could stop his feeling of panic because Felicity wasn't here. Everything about Mascatti—if it were Mascatti—was smooth and clever. "How did Kimble strike you?"

Jeremy turned to face him, still frowning.

"You know, Pat, I'm not soft. The hard-luck story just doesn't ring a bell with me. I thought I was proof against anything, but Kimble—he was pathetic. I was prepared to drop everything to help him. Fine job I've made of it, too."

"We've time," said Dawlish. "Tim, I'd like you to go and have a look at Kimble's home, as soon as you can."

"Right," said Tim.

Dawlish, at the window, saw a cyclist turn into the mews, and come up to the foot of the steps, and as he went to the hall he heard the lad whistling. The letter box opened, a letter dropped through and then the letter box clacked down again. The whistling faded. Dawlish picked up the letter, which was addressed to him in block capitals. He didn't like this, and he was deliberately slow in opening it; he mustn't panic. Jeremy, now in the hall, said:

"What is it?"

Dawlish ripped open the letter. There was a card inside. Dawlish glanced down at a photograph, and felt as if an electric shock had gone through his body.

It was of Felicity; and Felicity was asleep.

She seemed to be sitting up, her eyes were closed, her attitude completely relaxed.

Asleep?

Unconscious?

Dead?

The story of sleeping death flashed into his mind.

He turned the photograph over, and read the single pencilled sentence.

If you want her to wake up, keep out of this game.

CHAPTER XI

SCOTLAND YARD

Dawlish broke most road regulations on the way to Scotland Yard. He was *persona grata* there; only occasionally, and then for some special reason, had policemen denied him entry. He was greeted cheerfully by sergeants on duty, by plainclothes men in the corridors. He stopped at the door, tapped and thrust it open.

Superintendent William Trivett was standing by the side of his desk, hat still on, giving instructions to a young detective officer. He glanced round.

"Hallo, Pat. I won't be two jiffs. Take a pew."

"Thanks." But seconds might matter.

Trivett looked most people's idea of a City business man, and dressed the part. His suit was well-cut, he was good-looking in a formal way, dark-haired, alert. His voice was crisp as he finished his instructions. He turned to Dawlish as the door of the long, narrow room closed, and stopped abruptly.

"What's the trouble?"

"Felicity."

Trivett said, "Oh," in a strained voice. "What's happened?

I heard that you'd been pretty busy, but you must have been hitting hard."

"I don't know. I didn't think so." Dawlish talked in quick, terse sentences, and made the picture graphic. He did not name Carlotta or Kimble, but left out nothing else. Finally he handed the photograph across, and Trivett asked the first obvious question.

"How do you know it's not an old one?"

"She's wearing a brooch she bought in Paris last week."

"Clinches it," said Trivett.

"Yes. Bill, I don't feel so good. This business affected Tim and Ted far more than most of our shows. Rutter doesn't seem a big shot."

"Don't under-rate him," Trivett advised. He's better—or worse—than he looks."

"Then why's he free?"

"When Ted first mentioned him I knew it was a job you might tackle," Trivett said. "All I hear about Rutter are rumours. He's been on the fringe of a lot of unsavoury stuff. We've often questioned him, but never caught him on any charge. He looks small, seems to act and think small, and he's always the second-in-command, but that might be a blind."

"What about Percy Dipper?"

"He runs a little back-street gang, they never do anything much. Street book-making, hooliganism, car-snatching. We pick them up from time to time. Percy was inside for three months last year, and next time he'll get more. Going to charge him for attacking you with the knife?"

"Not yet," said Dawlish. "He might be useful. Mascatti?"

It was difficult to talk calmly; to get away from the nagging fear for Felicity, from the sight of her face, in complete repose, on the picture now in front of Trivett. He could call himself a fool, but it didn't help.

Trivett took his time answering.

"Mascatti is naturalized. He first came here twenty odd years ago, from Milan. He's run a number of restaurants, first as manager, later as owner. He owns at least six in London, and one or two in each of the big provincial cities. They're first class. The food's nearly perfect and the wines tip-top. He gives value for money. He does a lot for charity—especially helping displaced persons of Europe. Until Rutter joined him, I wouldn't even have thought of suspecting Mascatti of anything serious."

Trivett picked up Felicity's photograph. He didn't look at Dawlish. "This was probably privately developed. I'll try to find out. You know, Pat, we give you all the rope we can. Do you think you ought to use it, in this case? They could be serious." He was hedging.

Dawlish said heavily: "Come clean, Bill, What's this sleepy death—or sleeping death?"

Trivett went very still. They eyed each other, old friends—and old antagonists. Dawlish felt anxiety biting more deeply.

Trivett said deliberately: "So you're on to that. I don't know, it's accepted as a hitherto unknown illness. At least two of five men who died in their sleep worked for Rutter. The others are little crooks. I know nothing else. Do you?"

Dawlish said, "No." He didn't speak of Scotty or Dipper or refer again to the photograph of Felicity and the pencilled threat. He didn't want to admit the obvious.

He felt no better when he left. Because he hadn't mentioned Carlotta Morlay, and Kimble, he began to doubt his wisdom. It would be easy to take the girl and the doctor too much on trust. He wasn't sure how far he could go without help from Trivett, but decided that the moment wasn't ripe to go all the way.

He went to a telephone kiosk and called the Golden Shoe; Mascatti was in.

Dawlish said: "Listen. My wife's disappeared, and—"

"No!" exclaimed Mascatti. "Surely—"

"I said listen," repeated Dawlish heavily. "I've Dipper a prisoner, and you know what he thinks of you. If my wife isn't back within twelve hours, Dipper will talk to the police. I'll also tell the police about our little chat last night, and Kimble's disappearance. They know nothing about that, yet. Understand?"

"But, Mr. Dawlish—"

Dawlish rang off.

He drove back to the flat, without really expecting news; yet his heart thumped as he turned into the mews and he stared at the window.

Only Tim's face was against the window.

Tim opened the door for him.

"Anything?" Dawlish asked sharply.

"Nothing. I've spoken to everyone who might have seen something, but there isn't anything to help. Ted called. I told him about it, and he said he'd be right round. I've been trying to think, but can't get a line at all. It's been so—smooth."

"Right word," said Dawlish. "And if we really tried, we couldn't prove that anything had happened to Felicity, she might have walked out, run under a bus, done—" He caught his breath.

Jeremy said slowly: "The damnable thing is that we start thinking the worst before we've any idea whether it's justified. Nothing much has happened yet. No corpses."

Dawlish didn't speak.

A car sounded in the road nearby, slowing down. Dawlish was at the window in a flash. A two-seater sports car turned beneath the archway, and he looked for Felicity; and saw a youth. He was fair-haired, and fresh-faced, and the way he swept into the mews and stopped the car suggested that he knew all there was to know about driving. It was a vintage car, and looked as clean as a new pin.

The driver got out and looked up at the window.

He probably wasn't more than twenty-five or -six, and had a familiar look. His hair needed combing, and he brushed it back from his forehead impatiently. He wasn't happy, and showed it. He must have seen Dawlish, but showed no sign, just came up the steps, moving with the easy speed of an athlete, dressed in a sports coat and flannels. He disappeared from sight, and a moment later the front-door bell rang.

"Know him?" asked Jeremy.

"Kimble's son, I think—I've seen a photo. You open the door, will you?"

Dawlish waited in the room, with the door wide open, heard Jeremy's "Good morning," and the lad's response:

"'Morning. *You're* not Mr. Dawlish, are you?"

"No."

"Is he in?"

"Probably. Who are you?" Footsteps sounded in the hall.

"My name's Kimble. Terence Kimble. I want to see Dawlish. About—never mind, it's a private matter." His voice was taut, gave the impression that he was living on his nerves.

"All right, Tim," called Dawlish.

Kimble came in quickly. Jeremy followed, and Kimble said abruptly:

"This is confidential, Mr. Dawlish."

"Your father saw Mr. Jeremy yesterday, and told him all about the trouble," Dawlish said.

"Oh. That's all right, then." Terry Kimble walked across to Dawlish, and started to speak at once, words poured out of him. "I'm off my head with worry. My father hasn't been home since yesterday. He left yesterday afternoon, he was coming back to dinner, but he just didn't turn up. I thought there might be a message this morning, but there wasn't. I've telephoned round to all his clubs, and to everyone he might have stayed with. Drawn a blank. I'm—scared."

He started to speak, closed his eyes as if to shut out a vision, then seemed to draw himself up. He'd made some kind of decision.

What?

He lit a cigarette and his hand was unsteady. "*Are* you helping him?"

"I'm trying to."

Terry didn't look satisfied.

"I wish I knew whom I can trust. I thought you were all right, but—"

"Try me," said Dawlish.

"How much to you know?" Terry demanded.

"A story of blackmail and a man named Rutter—that's all."

Terry muttered: "That's about all I know, too. I've known that Dad's been worried for some time, but haven't known why. Then I wormed a bit of the truth out of him—he's being blackmailed. I'm sure it's that swine Rutter. Rutter visited us about once a month."

"What about Carlotta Morlay?" Dawlish asked.

Terry flashed, "What do you know about Miss Morlay?"

"Take it easy," said Dawlish. "I know you're good friends, and I know she works for Rutter. Or with Rutter. That's all." He lit a cigarette, and wondered what was really behind the expression in Terry Kimble's eyes. They were grey eyes flecked with green; and his hair was tinted with red. He looked as if he had a fiery temper—and a great weight on his mind.

"Sure that's all?" he demanded.

"From my side. What do you know about her?" asked Dawlish, and added mildly: "Sure you can trust her?"

Terry Kimble flushed a deep red, his fists clenched more tightly, he looked as if he would like to fling himself at Dawlish.

CHAPTER XII

ALARM

"Now look here," said Terry Kimble hotly, "if you're going to insult Miss Morlay, I may as well go. She's absolutely reliable. She's had a rough time, and if things had been normal at home she'd have been looked after when she reached here. As it is we've let her down. You can stop wondering about Carlotta."

"That's good. Now what about your father? Where did he go yesterday?"

"I don't know. That's the devil of it. He's been so secretive for weeks. Just said he was going out, and he hasn't come back. Do *you* know anything about it?"

"Not yet," said Dawlish. "Why don't you go to the police about all this?"

Terry muttered: "Because *he* won't. I begged him to. I can't understand what's the matter, but he's afraid of the police. Father's specialized and put everything into his work. Sunk a fortune. I happen to know that he is overdrawn heavily at the bank. He's practically ruined, because of this blackmailer. It's an absolute tragedy. I know this sounds corny," went on Terry, colouring, "but he's a good man. I don't care what anyone says, that's true. I'd do anything in the world to help him. You won't let him down, will you?"

"No. Has he been working with anyone lately?"

"Not regularly. People come and go. He always works on his own—says that at most stages of research it's better to have one man who's living in the research than several. One always leaves something to the other, in team-work. That's his idea, anyhow."

"Has he been on anything new lately?"

Terry threw up his hands.

"I just wouldn't know. He seldom talked about his work with me. He has a laboratory at the top of the house, and hides himself there. I've known him stay up there day and night for a week, before now. No, he's not there this time, I've looked. Everything's normal, as far as I can see."

"Didn't he have any assistants?"

"If he did, he brought them in for a special job, and then let them go. He does most of the donkey-work himself. I'm damned if I can see the point of all these questions, though. What has his work to do with blackmail?"

"That's what I'm trying to find out." Dawlish lit a cigarette and watching the young man judged that he was really in desperate straits. "I'm not there yet."

"I know," said Terry miserably. "Well, I might as well be off." He turned to the door, reached it before Dawlish, and then swung round. "About Carlotta. You don't seriously think she's working *against* my father, do you?"

The easy answer was the kindest. "No," said Dawlish.

"Thanks." Terry turned on his heel, and didn't seem to be able to get out of the flat quickly enough.

Jeremy saw him out and Dawlish watched him drive off. He didn't look round. Once he reached the street he put his foot down hard and the car roared towards Oxford Street. Jeremy came back, and said morosely:

"Silly young pup. You were too lenient."

"Could be," conceded Dawlish. "Oh, have a look at Dipper, will you? I moved him to the room leading off the garage."

"Right," said Jeremy.

Neither of them mentioned Felicity.

Dawlish rang the front-door bell of the house in the humble part of Paddington where he had talked to Carlotta. A receptionist in starched white cap and apron answered the door. Yes, Dr. Farningham was in, and not engaged, Mr. Dawlish could go straight in. Dawlish went into the surgery and Farningham, a well-built man whose black hair was going grey at the temples, looked up through horn-rimmed glasses, and put down his pen. He had some case-record cards in front of him.

"Hallo, Pat."

"'Lo, Bill." Dawlish sat down.

In some ways he felt closer to this man than to Beresford and Jeremy, although it was years since Bill Farningham had married and settled down to a general practice. He had practised in several districts, from London's more expensive suburbs to the East End, and now seemed content in this poor district. He was known as a first-class doctor; and was frequently at St. Mary's Hospital, not far away. In spite of his greying hair and the lines at the corners of his eyes and mouth he had a youthful look.

He frowned.

"What's up, Pat?"

"Felicity's missing," said Dawlish.

Farningham said, "Oh, the devil!" That was all; and it was enough.

Dawlish said briskly: "Moping won't help. The thing I don't

like about this case is the shortage of information. Even about Kimble. How much do you know of him?"

"Just that he's a brilliant research man."

"Know him personally?"

"Slightly." Farningham took off his glasses and rubbed his eyes. "He always kept himself pretty much to himself. When he wanted help he'd call on someone from one of the hospitals or the colleges, and he never had help from the same man more than once. Except one man," Farningham went on thoughtfully. "Young Ilott. Ilott helped him two or three times during the war, and I believe he's been helping him lately."

"Can you find Ilott for me?"

"I could," said Farningham. "I don't know whether I should, you'd be wiser to find him for yourself. He's not normal."

"What's the matter with him?"

Farningham laughed, shortly. "Just a freak. Not a single idea in his head, except about research. The completely detached scientist. Tall scarecrow of a chap, who doesn't think anyone outside the medical profession has a right to live. Nothing of Kimble's humanism about Ilott, he's just a cold-blooded analyst. I've never known anyone who knew and liked him. Kimble uses him more than anyone else—Kimble would find excuses for him. That's Kimble all over."

"Where can I find this Ilott?" asked Dawlish.

"I can get you his address. Take it from me, an introduction won't be any good. And he's the type who'll bang the door in your face if he doesn't like the look of you." He rang a bell, and the receptionist came in. "Get me Dr. Vernon Ilott's address, will you?"

"Yes, Doctor."

Farningham put his glasses back again, pushed cigarettes across the desk, and studied Dawlish thoughtfully. It wasn't the first time that Dawlish had been attacked through Felicity, so it wasn't the first time that Farningham had seen the bleakness in his face.

"I'm desperately sorry about Fel. Anything I can do?"

"Yes." Dawlish took out the sheet of paper which he had found in Kimble's wallet, and handed it across the desk. "That's Kimble's. He tucked it away when he was at the flat, obviously to stop anyone else from getting it. Think you can translate?"

Farningham glanced down, paused, and said:

"It'll take an hour or two. Can I hold on to it?"

"Guard it with—"

The telephone bell rang, and Dawlish broke off. The call was almost certainly for Farningham, yet he could not prevent the tensing of his muscles; it might be a message for him.

Farningham lifted the receiver. "Hallo." He hesitated. "Oh, hallo, Tim. Yes, he's here. Just a moment."

Dawlish almost snatched the telephone.

"Yes, Tim?"

"Had a message of sorts," said Jeremy quietly. "I can't be sure it's about Fel, but I fancy it is. No name, just some orders. You're to be at a certain place, alone, at four o'clock this afternoon. I—"

"What place?"

"Hounslow West Underground Station," said Tim Jeremy. "Much menace, Pat." He tried to speak lightly. "The usual stuff— if you don't go alone, if anyone else is seen with you or following you, then the responsibility for the consequences is yours, and Felicity won't wake up."

Dawlish said, "How did it come?"

"Telephone."

"Man or woman?"

"A man. I should say he spoke through a handkerchief or a scarf, his voice was muffled, there wasn't a chance of placing it.

It wasn't a long-distance call. He didn't waste much time—and he's given you plenty of notice, anyhow. Er—Pat."

"Yes?"

"The part about Fel was emphatic."

"I see. Anything else?"

"No."

"I'll be back before I go to Hounslow," Dawlish said. "Been to Kimble's place yet?"

"Yes. Nothing wrong, as far as I could see."

Dawlish rang off, as the door opened and the receptionist came in. "Might be news, might not be," he said abruptly. "I'll give these people one thing—they get properly under my skin."

"I've noticed that," said Farningham. "Is that the address, Nurse? Put it down, will you? Thanks." He took his glasses off again and went on quietly: "Pat, take it easy. You're looking as if you'll blow up if you keep up the pressure. And don't take chances."

Dawlish said mildly: "No. Thanks, Bill."

"I might as well talk to a brick wall," growled Farningham. "Well, here's Ilott's address." He glanced at the card, and read, "26, Fortescue Road, Hounslow."

Dawlish said softly: "Well, well! Where I'm to be this afternoon."

CHAPTER XIII

HOUNSLOW

Beresford and Jeremy were together at the flat, and the remains of a hurried cold meal were on the living-room table. Both men had tankards of beer on small tables by the side of their chairs. Dawlish dropped into his, and Beresford said:

"Sandwich?"

"Good thought. I forgot my snack."

"Fancied you would," said Beresford, and went towards the door. "Tell him, Tim."

Dawlish sat up as Jeremy went to the corner cupboard for beer and a tankard. Jeremy was looking much better, his eyes were no longer bloodshot, and he looked fresher, although still morose.

"Tell me what?" Dawlish demanded.

"This chap has some odd ideas, whoever he is," said Jeremy, pouring out. "There's a nice head for you. There was another telephone message. I'm to be at Chiswick station at four o'clock. Ted's to be at Hampstead Heath. No explanation given, just dark threats. Which means—"

"He wants to search the flat."

"Even I'd thought of that," said Jeremy tartly. "Going to let him search?"

"Yes."

"Who'll watch?"

"No one," said Dawlish quietly.

Jeremy looked as if he wanted to argue, but he didn't.

Dipper, less sleepy now, was back in the flat when Dawlish left at half past two; the others were to leave later.

Dawlish drove straight to Hounslow, but not to the West station. Fortescue Road was not far from the Heath, where red buses lumbered over roads once beaten to dust by coach and four, and where small boys threw stones, where highwaymen had fired matchlock pistols.

It was a bright, warm day. The heath looked fresh and green and the fringe of houses round it more attractive, in the sunlight, than they usually were; Fortescue Road was a turning off it—and not what Dawlish expected. There were several large houses, each standing in its own grounds, fifty years old or more. Most of the gardens had an unkempt look; none was so bad as Number 26.

This was a big, red brick house, hideous in design and made more hideous by a dead creeper which still clung to the walls over the big front door, although there were no leaves or flowers on it. The short drive was overgrown with weeds, the grass of shrubberies on either side had not been cut this year; and the bushes were wildly overgrown. As Dawlish walked from the street, where he left his car, he heard the fierce barking of a dog. As he neared the front door, a big mongrel came bounding from the back, still barking furiously.

"Good dog," said Dawlish, and went on walking. It snarled and leapt at him. He put out a foot and it crashed against his shoe and dropped back, still snarling. "I don't like doing it," said Dawlish in a casual voice, "but if you come again, you'll get more." He turned his back on the brute and stepped on to the big porch. The dog growled but he didn't come nearer. Dawlish pulled the big, old-fashioned pull-type bell and heard it clanging, just inside the front hall.

It was a little after three o'clock.

The dog still growled and the echoes of the bell lasted for a long time.

No one answered.

He rang the bell once more. The dog barked; that was all. He moved back, and the growling started again, he was sure that the brute would leap if he went back to the drive. He gave the bell a powerful tug, then thundered on the iron knocker. The dog was silent.

Nothing happened.

Dawlish turned and went down the steps. The dog backed away. Dawlish went to the side of the house, saw the side door standing open, and doors of the garage, which were ajar. He might have passed the garage had he not caught sight of the car inside. He could only see part of it, but it looked familiar. He opened the garage doors wide, and saw Terence Kimble's car; next to it, for the garage was large, was a little Baby Austin.

Dawlish turned towards the side door as a man appeared. If Farningham hadn't warned him, he would not have suspected that this was Vernon Ilott. Ilott was a tall, thin man with long hair, a beard and thick moustache, a pair of thick-lensed glasses. He had a lean and hungry look, and his eyes glittered behind the glasses. His lips were thin and his cheeks gaunt. He wore a pair of flannel trousers hoisted so high that the bottoms seemed halfway up his calves, a striped shirt and braces.

"What the devil do you want?" His voice was unexpectedly deep.

"To see Dr. Ilott."

"Seen enough?" Ilott growled.

"Nearly," said Dawlish. "If you're Ilott, you'll be wise to keep your dog under control."

"Damn your impudence. I need a watch-dog. Too many burglars and prying strangers about. I can't waste time with you."

"Who said anything about wasting time?"

"*I* did. Who are you? What do you want?"

"My name is Dawlish," said Dawlish; but his name seemed to mean nothing. "I'm looking for Dr. Kimble."

"He's not here."

"May I come and look?"

Ilott glared. "You can go back the way you came, and if you don't hurry, I'll set the dog on you."

Dawlish said, "I don't think we're going to get on, Dr. Ilott." He moved forward, and the dog growled. Ilott barred the way into the house; unless he moved, they would collide. Dawlish would have liked to keep an eye on the dog, but it was behind him.

Ilott moved aside, slowly, reluctantly.

"I haven't time for you."

"You can make time."

Dawlish reached the door and stepped inside. The dog snarled. The passage beyond was narrow, the walls wanted painting, and there was threadbare linoleum on the floor; yet everything seemed fresh and clean. He passed the kitchen door and caught a glimpse of an old-fashioned kitchen, with a big dresser and a deal table. The passage led to the hall through a swing door.

He stood in the hall.

Ilott came after him, in a towering rage.

"You've got a nerve! If you don't—"

"Oh, shut up," said Dawlish impatiently. "You work for Kimble, don't you?"

"I work for no man but myself."

"Why lie?"

Ilott said, "Get out of my house!"

"Later. Unless you want me to go and fetch the police at once."

Ilott said thinly, "The police have no more right here than you have."

"They'd have a right, if I tell them that Kimble's missing and I've reason to think he's here."

"He's not here. I haven't seen him for weeks. Well, days." Ilott's voice was still arrogant, but he was weakening, didn't quite know what to make of the visitor. "I don't know that he's missing, either. His silly fool of a son came babbling about it this morning, but I've no more time for him than I have for you. I've work to do."

"Where is Terry now?"

"I don't know."

"His car's in your garage."

"I told him he could leave it there."

"So you had a little time for him," said Dawlish. "Where can we go and have a chat?"

He thought that Ilott was going to refuse; saw the sudden indecision, and knew that his tactics were yielding dividends. Ilott turned without a word, and led the way into a big, sparsely furnished room at the front of the house. It was a drawing-room, with old-fashioned furniture of good quality, but so little of it that the room seemed empty. The Persian carpet was faded. Drawn curtains made it gloomy.

"Say what you want to say and make it snappy," Ilott said.

Dawlish sat in a saddle-back chair which was just too narrow for him, and wedged him at the shoulders. He eased forward, took out cigarettes and offered them.

"I don't smoke those poisonous things."

"Mind if I do?" Dawlish lit up. "Dr. Ilott, I don't know why you've greeted me like this, and I don't greatly care—unless you know something about Kimble's disappearance. Do you?"

"No!" the man shouted.

"Are you working with him at the moment?"

"No. And I'll never work with him or with anyone else again." Ilott's voice was filled with restrained fury; this wasn't simply boorishness, the man was bitter, and in a bubbling mood of anger. "Didn't I tell you I only work for myself?"

"What upset you?"

"That's my business."

Dawlish said wearily: "Oh, give it a rest. Why did you leave Kimble? Did he throw you out? Or hadn't he enough money to pay you?"

Ilott's thin lips quivered with anger, his bony hands clenched, he was just as aggressive as Terry had been. But he answered.

"If work's worth doing, I don't care about money. That's all you people can think of. Money, money, money! If you had to live off the soil and work with your own two hands instead of keeping them lily-white, I'd have some time for you. Man's become soft, pampered, empty-headed—like vermin. Or parasites. Each man lives off his neighbour, all of them are always wondering who they can swindle next. Money—don't think *I* use that measurement."

Dawlish didn't speak.

Ilott said heavily: "I left Kimble because he couldn't concentrate, couldn't give his mind to his work. He was always dashing out, always had something better to do. It was tragic—and maddening. Understand me? Maddening. I warned him time after time and it made no difference, so I walked out."

"When was this?"

"A month ago."

"Yet you've seen him since."

Ilott sneered. "He came here a week ago, begging me to go back. I showed him the door."

"You're good at showing people the door," said Dawlish dryly. "Was he working on something new?"

"That's a professional secret."

"You can tell me if it were new or not."

"Oh, all right," growled Ilott. "You won't understand, anyway. We were working on a synthetic formula for plasma. Blood, for transfusion. The present method is clumsy, takes too much time and needs the co-operation of too many people. Kimble's clever, I'll say that for him, when he puts his work first there's no one to beat him. Thanks largely to Kimble, we found that blood plasma can be stored for long periods in concentrated form but we want somehow to make the plasma. Kimble just stopped working on it, to all intents and purposes. Now *I'm* working on it—if you don't mind." He sneered.

"Not at all. Is that everything?"

"That," said Ilott thinly, "is a big enough problem to take him two or three years, even with *my* help. I don't think he'll ever finish it, he's gone soft. I—"

He broke off, for a bell pealed out, nearby; the big pull-bell. He glared towards the door. Dawlish had heard no footsteps, had been too intent on what Ilott was saying.

Ilott stood up.

"I'd better see who it is. Everything happens when I'm here by myself." He went out of the room swiftly, Dawlish could imagine him pulling the door open and growling:

"Well?"

A girl answered in a voice Dawlish wasn't likely to forget.

"Dr. Ilott please?" asked Carlotta Morlay.

CHAPTER XIV

RETURN

Dawlish was taken so completely by surprise that he forgot to expect an eruption from Ilott. He recovered a little, before Ilott spoke, and moved towards the door; it opened the wrong way to enable him to look out without being seen. Ilott was still silent—until the girl was spurred to ask sharply:

"Please. Are you Dr. Ilott?"

"Eh? Oh, yes. Yes, that's me. Dr. Ilott," said Ilott. The mixture of his deep voice and unexpected diffidence could have been funny, had Dawlish been in a mood to appreciate it. "*I'm* Dr. Ilott," continued Ilott, and then burst out: "Do you want me?"

This was better than Tim Jeremy drunk.

"I have brought you a letter from Mr. Mascatti," said Carlotta. "I do not know if there is any reply."

"Letter," said Ilott. "Oh. Mascatti. Don't know anyone named Mascatti." He paused. "Do I? Er—do come in, don't stand there on the doorstep. Won't keep you long." There were footsteps, and then: "Thank you, over here. I—" The footsteps drew nearer, and then Ilott's voice rose sharply. "No! Sorry. Wrong room. Er—this room." The footsteps went further away, another door opened, and all sounds faded.

Dawlish went into the hall smoking a second cigarette; he didn't realize he'd lighted it. The others had gone into a room at the far end of the passage. He passed by an open door, of the dining-room, as barely furnished as the other. The door of the third room was ajar, and he heard a rustle of paper; Ilott had taken his time opening that letter. Dawlish angled himself so that he could see in. Ilott was reading intently, the girl, standing profile towards Dawlish, was watching him—and smiling.

Dawlish fancied that she was really amused. Was she adult enough to be amused by the remarkable effect of her coming upon Ilott? Had she realized how out of character it was?

Ilott finished, looked up, coughed nervously, and said:

"Very nice of you to bring this. Thank you. I'm terribly sorry, but I can't accept. I'm extremely busy—significant research— don't feel I can work with anyone else anyhow—thanks very much." He mumbled. "Like me to write a note saying so? Terribly sorry. Er—who *is* Mr. Mascatti?"

That could be a genuine question; or it could be to fool Dawlish into believing that he and Mascatti weren't acquainted. Ilott's peculiar behaviour might be explained by the fact that he had been taken off his guard when the girl called with Dawlish here. Ilott didn't strike Dawlish as being a good conspirator.

"He is a night club and restaurant owner," said Carlotta.

"*Night* club?" Ilott exploded. "The man's a fool. Expecting me to work for the owner of one of those abominations!" This was the original Ilott, and sounded more real. "What a way to earn a living! Night clubs. Preying on the—" He broke off, and his gaunt face took on a look of acute embarrassment. "Er—I mean to say—"

"Folly of the people," suggested Carlotta.

"Good Lord! You see what I mean? Not many women would. If there's anything that makes me angry," went on Ilott, waving the letter in the air, "it's men who spend their lives in riotous living and encourage others. Drink—smoking—gambling—dancing—"

"Don't you do any of those things?" asked Carlotta. She appeared to be enjoying this.

Ilott waved the letter.

"Occasionally a glass of claret, occasionally a brandy. Perhaps a good cigar. In their proper place and of the right quality, they're all right, but the abortions—I beg your pardon."

"That's perfectly all right," said Carlotta gravely.

"Thank you." Ilott waved the paper again, then seemed to think of something he'd forgotten, and lowered it. "Yes. Well, tell Mr. Mascatti I'm far too busy to accept his—er—his kind offer."

"Yes, I will."

"Ah, thanks," said Ilott, and moved towards the door. Dawlish backed swiftly into the empty dining-room and stayed there. Ilott was bending down, being much taller than Carlotta, and saying: "Very glad you called. Most refreshing to meet an intelligent young woman. Any intelligent woman, for that matter. I—er—you—ah—you work for this Mr. Mascatti, do you?"

"Yes."

"At—er—at a night club."

"Oh, no. In his office."

"Oh, I see. I understand. Yes. Tell him I'm sorry, won't you?" Ilott opened the door and stood on the porch while the girl went off. Thus he gave Dawlish time to go back into the other room. Dawlish was waiting patiently, when Ilott came in again. Ilott had a rather dazed look; the change in him was so marked that it could hardly be genuine.

It was now a quarter to four.

"Sorry I left you," said Ilott. "Had an unexpected caller." He looked out of the window, and stuffed the letter into his pocket. "Now, what were we talking about? Oh, yes, Kimble's work. The truth about Kimble," he went on more loudly and aggressively, "is that he seems to have forgotten how to concentrate. Never seen such a change in a man. I simply can't work with him. He's one of the few men I could ever work with. Bound to be an Achilles' heel somewhere. Didn't you say something about him being missing?"

"Yes."

"Doesn't surprise me," said Ilott darkly. "Wouldn't surprise me to know that he's wandering about somewhere with amnes— that is, loss of memory. Shown signs of that lately, on several occasions. Unmistakable. Drops off to sleep, wakes up and doesn't realize that he's been asleep. That is one of the reasons why I left him, I didn't feel that I could work with a man who might sleep through an important part of the day's work. Do you blame me?"

"Not at all," said Dawlish, and stood up. "Thanks, you've been very good," he added solemnly.

"Not at all." That was an echo."

"I'll have to be going," said Dawlish.

He manœuvred to one side of the research man, and as they reached the front door, slipped Mascatti's letter out of his pocket. Ilott noticed nothing—and forgot himself so far as to shake hands. As Dawlish stepped on to the gravel, he heard a dog growl, but it wasn't in sight. A woman said:

"Be quiet, you noisy brute, be quiet." It was an elderly voice, and there was no venom in the words. Presumably Ilott's house-keeper was back, and had the dog under control.

Ilott did not wave from the porch.

Dawlish sat at the wheel of his Rolls-Bentley and read Mascatti's letter. It was short and to the point. He said that he was anxious to have some experimental research work carried out privately, he had heard of Dr. Ilott's reputation, and if Dr. Ilott were free, would be happy to appoint him at a salary which he was sure would be satisfactory. Obviously Mascatti wanted his services; as obviously, Ilott had told the truth when he had said that he wasn't interested in money for its own sake.

If Mascatti were behind the instructions to Dawlish and the others, he would expect Dawlish to be on his way to the station, would not expect him to be with Ilott. There could have seemed little risk in sending Carlotta as a messenger; in fact there had been no visible risk.

Why did Mascatti want Ilott?

To work with Kimble? Or to go on with Kimble's experiments where he had left off?"

Dawlish put speculation behind him and drove to the station at Hounslow West. It was a modern station, the low-built building showed against the clear blue sky, with its environment of small detached and semi-detached houses.

Dawlish pulled up outside the station at one minute past four.

At one minute past five he was still there.

In the interval, he had plenty of time to wonder whether he should have had the flat watched. He could not have explained why he had felt it essential to do exactly as he had been told. A kind of hunch; in kindlier moments, Felicity would have called it the operation of his sixth sense. He wasn't feeling as if any senses were working at all. Anxiety for Felicity, lulled by the message and by the visit to Ilott, had stormed back.

He decided to wait until a quarter past five.

At ten minutes past a lad came cycling up, wearing a school cap and a satchel on his back. He came across to the Rolls-Bentley and touched his cap.

"'Afternoon, sir."

"Hallo," said Dawlish.

"Are you a Mr. Dawlish?"

"That's right."

"I met a man down the road, sir, and he asked me to give you a message. He said there wasn't any need to stay any longer, and that you'd know what I meant. Hope you do." He smiled ingenuously.

Dawlish said slowly: "Yes, I know. What was the man like?"

"Well—like almost anyone, I suppose. Ordinary, I mean. There wasn't anything special about him. He was in a little Austin—brand new model, too, but not a patch on this. *Wonderful* job, isn't it?" he enthused.

"Not bad," said Dawlish. "Not bad at all, in fact." He handed the lad half a crown. "Thanks a lot."

The boy went off, cheerfully.

Dawlish didn't understand it and didn't try.

He tried to get back to the flat quickly. He was unlucky—homeward traffic was too thick. It was nearly a quarter past six when he reached the mews. He expected to see one or both of the other cars, but they weren't there. With so much warning, Tim and Ted could look after themselves, there was nothing to worry about.

Except Felicity.

He got out of the car and went to the foot of the steps, glanced up—and saw Felicity at the window.

CHAPTER XV

FELICITY CHIDES

Dawlish stood quite still. Felicity looked normal and natural, waved and disappeared. She was coming to open the door. Dawlish started slowly up the steps. His relief was so great that he couldn't think clearly. He wasn't thinking clearly when he reached the door as it opened, and Felicity smiled.

He crushed her to him; and they stood together for a long time. She muttered a muffled "Pat!" and he let her go and stared at her tensely.

"Darling, don't suffocate me," she said.

"Are you—all right?" His voice was gruff.

"Of course I'm all right. What's the matter with you?" She looked fresh and lovely. She wore the same clothes and the brooch which she had bought in Paris she had just made up; much as she might look after an afternoon's rest. "Are *you* all right?"

"Er—I think so." They went in. "I wont be a moment," he said, and went to the room where Dipper had been left. Dipper wasn't there. Dawlish went back to Felicity, knowing he'd needed a few moments away from her, to get back on an even keel.

"What happened?" he asked.

Felicity frowned. "What happened where? Pat, what's the matter with you?"

"Matter with *me!*" gasped Dawlish. "Where have you been? If you tell me that you went out to do some shopping and decided—"

"Listen, darling," said Felicity, putting a cool hand on his arm and leading him into the living-room, "a joke's a joke, and we've had enough of this one."

Dawlish uttered a single, strangled word.

"*Joke?*"

"I agree, not everyone would think it funny," conceded Felicity, "but I know your little ways. How are things going? Have you had any luck?"

Dawlish dropped into a chair. "Some would say so. Can you reach the whisky?"

"What's the matter with beer?"

"I need something stronger," said Dawlish faintly. "A double and a splash. No more than a splash."

Felicity's face had a serenity which she often showed when in repose, and when she was thoroughly contented. She went to the corner cupboard and he watched her pour out whisky. One of the things easily forgotten about Felicity was her ease of movement, her grace in trivial things. She turned towards him and brushed a strand of hair out of her eyes.

"There you are," she said. "I suppose you're wondering what's for lunch."

Dawlish nearly dropped the glass.

"*Lunch?*"

"That's right, my pet. Pat, you're talking as if you didn't quite know where you are. Aren't you hungry? I know you had a good breakfast, but you're usually ravenous by now. Unless you've been eating while you've been out." She was ready to be disapproving; not very disapproving, though, something had greatly mellowed her.

Dawlish drank deeply.

"My sweet," he said, "I can't stand much more of this. The time is now . . ." He looked at the clock on the mantelpiece before he spoke. This time he actually let the glass slip, grabbed, saved all but a little; that little spilt on to his trousers and slowly soaked in.

The hands of the mantelpiece clock pointed to twenty minutes to one.

He groaned. "Oh, no!"

"What *is* the matter?" Felicity was becoming anxious. "Pat, are you well? You're not looking too good, you look dazed. What's happened? Why were you so long?"

Dawlish said heavily: "Oh, this and that. Yes, I'm all right. Never better."

She didn't know she'd been away; why tell her, now? Why worry her? And why add the task of explaining fully when so much pressed on his mind? He could leave it.

He drained his glass as he stood up.

"Nothing happened here, I suppose?"

"No. Tim went out, looking like death. I don't think he's forgiven himself for last night, although he was obviously doped, like you were supposed to be. Ted rang up, Tim told him there was nothing to bring him here yet, said you'd ring if you wanted him. I've a steak casserole in the oven, I'll go and see how it's getting on."

She went out.

Dawlish mopped his forehead, stared at the door, and then looked at his own watch. It was twenty-five minutes past six. He went into the bedroom; a table clock there tallied with the mantelpiece clock; so did another, in the second bedroom. He actually peered through the kitchen doorway and saw the time by the frying-pan clock in there; twelve minutes to one. Someone had altered them all.

Dawlish went back to the living-room, lighting a cigarette, and then heard a car draw up. He opened the door and hurried down the steps. Tim was getting out of his Riley; a thunderous-browed Tim. He glowered as Dawlish reached him.

"Satisfied *now*? It was a fool's errand. I hung about for over an hour, and then a kid came up and told me I needn't wait any longer. A schoolboy! He knew my name, said someone had asked him to give me the message. I felt murderous. I *feel* murderous. And I want a drink. What are you standing there for?"

Dawlish said: "Listen, Tim." He paused, and Jeremy saw that he was serious. "Dipper's gone and Felicity's back. Unharmed. She doesn't know she's been out. I'm going to keep that up. She's obviously been drugged, she's quite happy at the moment and I'm going to let things ride with her."

"*What?*" breathed Tim.

"That's it. I—" Dawlish broke off, hearing the familiar sound of Ted's car. "Wait a minute, and I can tell you both together." He watched Ted drive in, his brow as thunderous as Tim's, but with more evidence of anxiety. He came over quickly.

Dawlish talked.

They couldn't believe him.

He said: "I think we ought to let Felicity stay as she is. If recollection comes as the evening wears on, it'll reduce shock effect. If she's told that she had knockout drops which put her out for six or seven hours, and she just didn't know, she's bound to be affected."

Jeremy said, "This is uncanny."

"They mean it to be."

"Only word," agreed Beresford. "So they wanted us out so that they could take Dipper and bring her back."

"It could be that they just wanted to bring Felicity back. To show how they can do their stuff. Listen—Felicity has lunch nearly ready. We'll have it as if it were really lunch-time, and I'll slip her some veronal. With luck, she'll sleep well from it, wake up, and be ready for the story. We can alter the clocks when she's asleep. All right?"

They played their parts manfully.

"Darling," said Felicity, just after seven o'clock by the real time, "I think I'll have a nap this afternoon. I suppose I'm feeling the reaction from Paris." She yawned. "Are you going out?"

"One of us will be here," promised Dawlish.

"Don't be out late yourself," said Felicity. One of the odd things was that she appeared to have lost all anxiety about the case. "Oh, and about that man in the small room."

"Ah, yes. Percy Dipper."

"You can't let him stay there indefinitely. I know you feed him, and all that, but you can't keep a prisoner too long."

"You have your nap—I'll look after him," said Dawlish. "Like a cup of tea first?"

"Well . . ."

He made tea, and slipped the sleeping draught into her first cup. In spite of being tired she had the same look of serenity. Perhaps it was because she had been missing, but she had become more precious. He stared at her from the door, and she laughed and waved him away.

"Don't let me sleep too long, darling."

"I won't!"

He closed the door and went into the big room. This was the first opportunity he'd had of talking to the others. Twenty minutes later they knew as much as he did about Ilott and the offer from Mascatti; and about Terry Kimble's odd behaviour.

"That young man wants watching," Tim said. "He's not so young and foolish as he looks."

"True. Your job," said Dawlish.

"Seriously?"

"Oh, yes."

"Right!" said Tim. "That reminds me—I didn't get far in Kimble's place. Looked round a bit, but—"

"We'll take a longer look tonight."

"Okay." Tim went out, and had hardly closed the door when the telephone bell rang. Dawlish was near enough to reach it without getting up. Beresford, leaning back in the other outsize armchair, was smoking and frowning.

"Hallo."

"Mr. Dawlish?" It was Carlotta.

"Hallo, Carlotta!"

"There's something I have to tell you. I had to go and see a Dr. Ilott this afternoon. Dr. Vernon Ilott. It's an unusual name. He lives at 26, Fortescue Road, Hounslow. I took him a letter, offering some work, and he refused it. Mascatti wasn't at all pleased. I thought you should know."

"You've never been more right," said Dawlish.

"I don't know what the work was. This Dr. Ilott is a peculiar man." She broke off, then asked, "Is there—is there any news?"

"Not yet."

"Please find him," said Carlotta.

Dawlish heard the receiver go down, turned and looked at Beresford thoughtfully, told him the gist of the message, and was lighting a cigarette when the front-door bell rang. It was getting dark now; he hoped the sleeping draught had worked with Felicity.

Bill Farningham was at the door.

"Hallo, there." Dawlish stood aside for him to come in. "Quite like old times. Ted's in, Tim's out." They joined Ted. "Beer?"

"Thanks."

"I'll pour," said Beresford. "Usual head?"

"Nothing's changed," said Farningham, smiling, but that didn't stop him from looking tired. "Well, I've been through that sheet of hieroglyphics, Pat."

"Anything?"

"I shouldn't think it would have anything to do with Kimble's disappearance; I can't see any money value in it. He was working on blood transfusion—plasma—wasn't satisfied with the present methods. He had a notion that a synthetic substitute could be found. This seems to be a sheet of notes explaining how it *doesn't* work."

"Doesn't?"

"Beer." Beresford handed over two foaming tankards.

"That's right—doesn't. It's not all there, of course, but I should say this was a summary of the final results of a long research—and it didn't work. Mind you, it's often necessary to start again from scratch, and that's what Kimble would do. I can't see why he should try to hide it from anyone. What else was in that wallet?"

Dawlish took the wallet out of his own pocket, glanced at the photographs and the rest of the contents, and could think of nothing that might explain anyone's interest.

"Mystery," he said, and put the contents back. "Thanks, Bill. Odd thing happened today." He told the story of Felicity's return.

"Well?" Dawlish almost barked the word when he had finished. "Any medical explanation?"

"Could be," said Farningham promptly. "It's a form of amnesia. There are ways of inducing it, with drugs. Usually the period lasts much longer than this—or else much less—as with the ordinary anæsthetic. She hasn't shown any after effects, so I would say it's a narcotic drug. It's a drug, all right. Say she's asleep now?"

"I gave her veronal, hoping she would sleep through the night."

"I'll go and have a look at her," said Farningham. He finished his beer and Dawlish led him into the hall, but didn't go into the room with him, for the front-door bell rang.

"I'll see you in a minute," he said, opening the bedroom door for Farningham and then the front door.

Dr. Vernon Ilott exclaimed, "Thank heavens I've found you!"

CHAPTER XVI

MURDER LOOKS IN

Ilott was breathing hard. The passage light fell on his black beard and moustache and made his eyes glint, but there was nothing ferocious about him. He stepped inside, Dawlish closed the door, and Ilott gripped his wrist with fingers which had a nervous strength.

"You are *the* Dawlish, aren't you?"

"Come in here," said Dawlish, and led the way into the living-room. "This is a friend of mine, Mr. Beresford. Ted, tell Bill I can't make it for a few minutes, will you, and stand guard in case he wants anything."

Ted went out.

"Aren't you?" cried Ilott. "*The* Dawlish?"

"I'm Patrick Dawlish, and I've helped the police occasionally, if that's what you mean."

"You're always getting your name in the papers. After you'd gone I realized it. I've seen your photograph." He clamped his lips together for a second, then burst out: "I need help. Desperately."

"What kind of help?"

Ilott drew a deep breath, raised a clenched hand, and said tensely:

"There's a dead man at my house."

Dawlish said slowly: "I don't get it. Dead?"

"Murdered," Ilott flung at him. "What on earth are you sitting there for? You're a detective, aren't you? I want help. My car's outside in the street. For heaven's sake, hurry; I can tell you about it on the way."

"I'll be five minutes," said Dawlish, and added abruptly: "My wife's ill; the doctor's with her now."

"Eh? Oh, I didn't know. I'm sorry. Look here, Dawlish, if you *can't* help—"

"I'll do what I can." Dawlish hurried out of the room, past Ted, who was leaning against the wall near the bedroom door, and into the bedroom. Bill Farningham was moving away from the bed. Felicity lay asleep, still fully dressed except that she had taken off the suit coat and kicked her shoes off.

"Anything?" Dawlish asked abruptly.

"Not a thing. Pulse and heart quite normal. She's sleeping under the veronal now. I could try a blood test and one or two other things, but doubt if it's necessary. She's perfectly all right."

"Fine! Think she'll sleep till morning?"

"Several hours, anyhow. I suppose you're anxious she shouldn't know what happened?"

"I want to break the news gently."

"Yes, you're right," said Farningham. "I'll make a few inquiries and find out if there's any new drug on the market. Might be something from the Continent or the U.S.A., but I haven't read about it in any of the medical journals."

"Thanks, Bill. Now I've got to rush." Dawlish went out with Farningham, who wouldn't go into the living-room again, but hurried off. Beresford was waiting patiently.

"Will you stay?" asked Dawlish. "Don't leave Fel, on any account."

"Right, old chap. By the way, where's Roger Brent?"

"Watching Carlotta."

Beresford grinned. "He isn't likely to complain about that. Any idea how long you'll be?"

"Say midnight," said Dawlish. "I'll either telephone or be back by then." He opened the living-room door and saw Ilott pacing up and down like a caged beast. "Ready?"

"Ready!" cried Ilott. "Of course I am. Dawlish, this is the most astonishing thing that ever happened to me. I was in the laboratory. Top of the house. My housekeeper only comes by day, she'd left before dinner—I had a cold dinner. Was relaxing for half an hour afterwards, and went back to the laboratory. This—this man was *there*."

They were at the foot of the steps.

"How long had you been out of the laboratory?"

"No more than an hour. It's a most astonishing thing." Ilott was halfway to the archway. "I told you my car's outside, didn't I?" Seldom had a man found it so difficult to suffer fools gladly. "He'd been stabbed with one of the instruments—dissecting instruments. Mine. I tell you, I was in a panic."

"Yes." They reached the street—and the tiny baby Austin which Dawlish had seen in the garage at Ilott's house stood by the kerb. "Get in," ordered Ilott.

"You drive back in your own car, and I'll follow. I'll arrive a few minutes after you. Don't go into the house until I've seen you again."

"Well—all right, if you think it's wise."

Dawlish turned away and saw Ilott climb into the baby car; he had to fold himself up like a knife but the engine purred sweetly. No one followed Dawlish when he drove off in the big car.

* * *

It was nearly eleven when Dawlish reached Fortescue Road. He didn't turn into the drive of Number 26, but into one three doors away, pulled the car into the side so that there was room for other cars to pass, then walked to Ilott's house. No lights were on. There was a half-moon, and he saw the shape of the baby Austin near the front of the house. There was no sign of the dog. Dawlish's footsteps crunched on the gravel as he approached— and a dark figure moved.

"Who's that?" called Ilott, and switched on a light.

He was standing just inside the radius of light, looking wild and aggressive; his beard was untidy and his eyes seemed to be glaring. He wasn't wearing his thick-lensed glasses.

"What are you fooling about at, Dawlish?"

"Trying to make sense of this," said Dawlish. "Did you kill the man upstairs? A lot of innocent people would call the police on finding a body."

"And have them tramping all over the place, asking sense-less questions, prying into my work, probably taking me off for more questioning? Not if I can help it! *That's* why I came to you. If the body is found somewhere else, no one will worry me about it, will they?"

"Well, well," said Dawlish. "Cooler than you'd think."

"I don't know what you're talking about. I wanted to see you, anyhow." Ilott blinked furiously, and reminded Dawlish of his behaviour with Carlotta. "Remember when you were here this afternoon someone called to see me? They left a letter, and I've lost it. I wondered if you'd seen it anywhere. I was going to find you, anyhow, because I want the address." Could that be for *Carlotta*? "Then I saw the body and—well, *I* don't want the police here. Be no need for police if people behaved properly, instead of living artificially." He licked his lips. "Aren't you going to see this man?"

"Good idea," said Dawlish. It was just possible that the man was as unworldly as he made out. Why was he anxious about that letter? Had he given the real reason for visiting the flat?

They began to walk upstairs.

"Ever seen the man before?" Dawlish asked.

"Complete stranger," said Ilott. "As a matter of fact—" He didn't finish but quickened his pace, and his long, lean legs moved very fast. At the second landing they went along a passage, then up another flight of steps, then into a room protected by a heavy door. Steel? Dawlish decided to find out later, and stepped inside.

Percy Dipper lay on the floor with a knife in his chest.

CHAPTER XVII

PRESSURE

Ilott, walking towards the body, might have been approaching a specimen preserved for surgical experiments.

"See? That's my instrument. Took it from over there." He pointed to a sterilizing tray of them in a corner. The room was large, a bench stretched all along one side, with a roof-light above it; northlight, probably, as an artist would require. Glass retorts, test-tubes, bottles, instruments and Bunsen burners littered the bench. There were pigeon-holes round the walls and most were completely filled; it was a cross between a science laboratory and a chemist's shop. The lighting was fluorescent strip, and gave Ilott's face a waxen look. "Went straight to the heart. Little external bleeding—just a seepage round the edge of the knife; often happens that way with a thin knife. Whoever used it knew where it was going. Won't bleed much, now—at least, it won't if it's left in much longer. Better to leave it; we don't want to make a mess."

"You're pretty cold-blooded," said Dawlish.

Ilott shrugged impatiently.

"Nonsense! Lot of sentimental twaddle talked about death.

Man was alive and is dead. He can't feel anything now, probably didn't feel more than a sharp prick when it went in. What I can't understand is why he was killed here, and what he was doing here."

"Any idea how he got in?"

"By the back door, I expect. There's a secondary staircase, up to the second floor—you saw it, didn't you? Easy enough, if I were at the front downstairs. I was looking for that letter."

"What was in this letter?"

"Offer of work," said Ilott promptly. "I couldn't accept. But I'd like the address. I believe it was a night club, I seem to remember there was a shoe on it, although what connection there is between a night club and a shoe I can't imagine. Can you?"

"There's a club called the Golden Shoe, run by a man named Mascatti."

"That's the man!" Ilott cried. "Mascatti. Golden Shoe—what's the address? Do you know?"

"If you don't want the job, why are you so anxious?"

"That's *my* business."

Dawlish said: "All right. You might look in a telephone directory for the address."

Ilott swung round, and Dawlish caught his arm.

"Later," he said firmly. "When a man's been murdered in your house that's the thing to worry about."

"But I'm employing you to look after that," said Ilott. "What more do you want? Fee in advance? Name it, and—"

Dawlish felt a rush of annoyance, then of amusement. He chuckled. Ilott blinked. Dawlish led him to a high stool by the bench, and perched himself on another. He lit a cigarette and said quietly: "Now listen, Ilott. You may be a scientist and above mundane things, but you're in a jam. This man was killed here and if the police find out they'll suspect you. Looking on police as vermin won't help you—in fact, it would probably do you a lot of harm. Understand?"

Ilott muttered, "Damned nuisance."

"That's right. Now try to think. Why was he killed here? Because someone wants the police to think you killed him."

"*What?*"

"Just turn it over in your mind."

Ilott placed his hands at his hips and drew up his legs so that they rested on a cross-strut of the stool. The light shone straight on to his glasses and glinted, making it difficult to see his expression.

"Not a fool," he said. "You think I am, but I'm not. Knew who you were when you called. Terry Kimble mentioned you. Said you were looking for his father. I denied I knew Kimble was missing. Didn't think you'd do any good. Then this happened. I'm *not* a fool. Couldn't imagine why a man I've never seen before should be killed in a way which looks as if I killed him. I 'phoned some friends who said you're pretty good, after all. Thought I'd come and see what you made of it. *Could* be a frame-up. That's the word. Frame-up. Is that what you're thinking?"

Dawlish said very slowly, "I don't believe you got that idea from the little you know."

Ilott shrugged.

"Know more than you think. Terry told me that his father was being blackmailed. *This* could be blackmail. Form of, anyway. Couldn't it? By the way, Terry didn't name me; I asked him not to. Young fool. I've lent him money, when he's been in a jam; he daren't let me down or he'd wonder if any more was coming. See how my mind worked?"

"Yes, I think so," said Dawlish, and smiled. "Not bad. So you're expecting someone to high-pressure you into accepting work for Mascatti, because of this."

"Could happen, couldn't it?"

"Yes. I want to know what work Mascatti can offer you."

Ilott grunted. "I don't know myself."

"You can find out," said Dawlish. "We'd probably get to the end of this business more quickly if you accepted the job. And we'd find Kimble and find out why Kimble was so worried. You've guessed that he couldn't keep on with his work because he was blackmailed, haven't you? Lost the power of concentration, because of it."

"Oh, yes," said Ilott. He climbed down from the stool and began to walk about. "Didn't want anything to happen to affect *me* that way. Kimble had mental black-outs!" His voice was shrill. "Still, he's been friendly towards me. Not many are. And . . ." He hesitated, then added abruptly, "Do you know Mascatti's secretary?"

"One of them," said Dawlish. "I know the girl who came here this afternoon, if that's what you mean."

Ilott sprang towards him.

"Did you see her? Sure? Know her?"

"She's Carlotta Morlay. She came here from Czechoslovakia, expecting help from Kimble which she didn't get. Mascatti employed her because she knew Kimble. I don't think she's in acute danger, but she might be. That's a possible reason for going to see Mascatti and finding out about this job."

"I'll go!" said Ilott abruptly. "I'll go right away. No sense in losing time, and—"

A bell rang shrilly. He glanced round in annoyance.

"That's the front door," he growled.

There was a hatch between the wall of the dining-room and a smaller room next door. With it open a few inches, Dawlish could hear what was said in the dining-room, where Ilott agreed to take the caller. Dawlish heard footsteps and Ilott's voice, followed by the unmistakeable voice of Rutter.

Rutter's voice was pitched on a low key and held a sneer. Everything that was bad about him seemed to reveal itself as he spoke. Dawlish heard every syllable, and could also hear Ilott's breathing.

"That's right, Dr. Ilott, I want to show you a picture of a dead man. Pretty picture, you'll agree. Now take it easy and don't get excited. You're an excitable guy, aren't you?" There was a pause, then Ilott exclaimed and Rutter chuckled. "Well, what do you think about it? You've been up there and seen all about it, haven't you? You know he's there. Look." There was another pause. "Recognize that knife? Yours, isn't it? If I tell the police you'd be in a bad way. If you'll take Mascatti's job, I won't tell—"

He broke off. Dawlish heard a thud, then a crash. He thought he heard Rutter gasp, bent down and looked through the partition. Rutter was lying on the floor, a chair lay on its side near him, and Ilott stood over him. Rutter had a hand at his mouth and lay glaring up.

Ilott growled: "Now get up. Get up! I'll knock you down again, you swine. Get up!" He actually bent down and grabbed Rutter's arm. Rutter didn't pull himself free—nor did he pull a weapon.

"*Get up!*"

"Now take it easy, Doctor," said Rutter thickly. "You aren't going to do yourself any good by going on like that. What do you want me to do? Call the police?"

"You won't be able to call the police by the time I've finished with you!"

"Take it easy," repeated Rutter. "I can call them and they'd find the body. In your lab, with your knife in his ticker. And something else, Doctor. Evidence that you and that dead man had been quarrelling. It would be built up so there was no way out for you. Like the idea?"

Ilott growled between set teeth, "Get up."

"When you're sensible. You don't have to have any trouble. Just do a little job, and you won't have to worry any more, Doctor. That photograph I've shown you will be destroyed, with the negative, and you won't have to worry. You'll get paid for it, too."

Ilott didn't speak. Rutter got to his feet warily and backed to a safe distance. He still dabbed at his bleeding lips.

"You'll get *well* paid, too. Be sensible. There's money where I come from."

Ilott managed not to sneer at the word money.

"What do you want me to do?"

"That's better—we'll get on fine if you keep on like that," said Rutter. "You know Dr. Kimble, don't you?"

"What if I do?"

"He's ill," said Rutter mockingly. "He was doing some important work and collapsed in the middle of it. You're to start where he left off. You know the way he works, don't you? It'll be easy for you. And look—fifty quid in advance." He took out an envelope and held it up—and again Ilott managed not to sneer at filthy lucre. "We tried the nice way and I heard what happened," Rutter went on, "so I had to try the nasty way. But you'll be all right if you'll do as you're told. Okay?"

Ilott said hoarsely: "Where do you want me to work?"

"That's the ticket! Not far away—not here, but in London. *Kimble's* place. He's got all the equipment you'll need, hasn't he? And you're a pal of his son's. Just arrange with his son to have the use of the lab, and he'll fix it. Then you'll be able to start work properly and Kimble won't have anything over you. But listen, Doctor. If you try any tricks, that photograph of the corpse will go to the police. I can frame you."

Ilott said: "You brainless fool, the police would want to know who took the picture and what he was doing there."

Rutter snapped: "Now listen—"

"Forget it. I'll work—but I want more than fifty pounds in advance. I want five hundred."

"*What?*"

"You're not deaf, are you?"

Rutter gulped.

"No, I'm not deaf. So that's it." He gave a shrill laugh. "You're better than I thought you were. Okay. Five hundred—the day you start working. That's tomorrow. Be at Kimble's place by half past ten, and have it all arranged with Terry Kimble. All clear, Doctor?"

"Get out of here," growled Ilott.

Rutter said: "Okay. I don't want to stay where I'm not wanted. But there's one more thing, Doctor. You might hear from a Mr. Dawlish. Don't say a word to him and don't say a word to anyone. So long."

CHAPTER XVIII

KIMBLE'S HOUSE

Dr. Vernon Ilott closed the front door of his house with a bang and turned to look at Dawlish. He looked on top of the world as he rubbed his bony hands together. There was nothing unworldly about him now. Dawlish smiled faintly as he came forward.

"Satisfied?" demanded Ilott.

"Very nicely handled. Can you fix it with Terry Kimble?"

"I've told you that he'll do whatever I want, he owes me too much—and I don't just mean money," said Ilott abruptly. "I'll telephone him tonight."

"Do that. Ask him to come and see you."

"There's no need—"

"Ask him," said Dawlish. "Is his car still in the garage here?"

"No, he took it away."

"Then he won't have any trouble getting here. Say you must see him at one o'clock," said Dawlish.

Ilott hesitated—then grinned.

"I see. You want to go and look through his house. I suppose there's no reason why I shouldn't oblige, but before you go, what about that body?"

"Keep it there or hide it until this job's over," Dawlish said flatly.

They hid the body in the attic, together.

Dawlish called at the first telephone kiosk on his way to London and dialled the Golden Shoe. Carlotta answered him. He asked for Mascatti.

"Who wants him, please?"

"Patrick Dawlish."

"Daw—" she began, and then stopped. "I see. I think he's in the club; I'll have to send for him. Will you hold on, please?"

"It wouldn't surprise me if he's with Rutter," Dawlish said. "He and Rutter will probably have an interesting chat tonight." He wondered if she would get what he was driving at; that he wanted her to try to hear what they said, but was reluctant to put it into so many words: someone else might be listening in.

"I won't keep you long." She sounded aloof.

He held on for three minutes. It was much colder than it had been lately, and he pulled his coat more tightly round him. The headlights of two or three cars caught the Rolls-Bentley. One car slowed down then went on again.

"Mr. Dawlish?" It was Mascatti. "I hope you have good news of your wife."

Dawlish said, "Oh." He hadn't expected the gambit; he wasn't at all sure of Mascatti. "Oh, yes," he added quickly. "Thanks. I haven't any time to spare now. This is my end of the bargain, and I'm keeping it."

"Yes, Mr. Dawlish, what is it?"

"Two things. Young Kimble begged me to help him last night. And this evening I had a call from a crazy coon named Ilott. Got that? Ilott. He said he needed help, was almost in tears when I said I wouldn't help him. I happen to know that Ilott and Kimble worked together one time."

"Mr. Dawlish," said Mascatti, "you're doing more than I could expect. Thank you."

"A bargain's a bargain," said Dawlish. "But listen—if you try any more tricks with me you'll see the other side."

"I don't understand you."

"Don't play the fool with my wife."

Mascatti said, "I know nothing at all about what happened to her."

Dawlish said heavily: "I'd like to believe you. Why did you get me away from my flat? And why take Percy Dipper away?"

"You're making a big mistake," said Mascatti. "I know nothing at all about either of those things."

"That had better be true," said Dawlish.

He rang off before Mascatti could speak again, stepped outside the box, and watched a motor-cyclist come tearing along the road; he couldn't have been doing much less than ninety. Dawlish went to his car, but didn't drive off immediately. The craziest thing would be to believe Mascatti; unless it would be crazier to take it for granted that Mascatti had lied.

Who was the bad man? Mascatti—or Rutter? Or an unknown? Dead Dipper had known.

Dawlish started the engine, let in the clutch and drove off. It was twenty minutes to one when he reached Gaw Road, St. John's Wood—where Kimble lived. He had the address, but didn't know that the house was at the far end of the street. He parked the car fifty yards off and walked to the house. There were no lights, and everywhere was quiet. His own footsteps made the only sound. He wasn't watched; hadn't been followed from Ilott's.

He didn't know how many servants were kept at the house,

and made a complete circuit of it before feeling sure that there were no lights on. Then he examined the windows. One at the back was open a few inches at the top—a small window, but he could squeeze through.

He pulled it down, hauled a garden seat beneath it, climbed up and through. He stood in the silent house for a few seconds and then began to explore. It was old-fashioned, almost as old-fashioned as Ilott's, but there was much more furniture. In a big drawing-room, where he turned on the lights after drawing the curtains, he saw three coloured photographs of an elderly woman—the woman whose snapshot he had seen in Kimble's wallet.

He made sure no one was downstairs, and went up. There were three storeys altogether. He found a bedroom which had obviously been used that night. Oddments showed that it was Terry Kimble's. The bed hadn't been slept in, but an ash-tray was full of butts. He found another bedroom, which he thought was Dr. Kimble's. A portrait of the woman was on the wall opposite the big double bed, and there were other pictures of her, in different poses. She was dead; but her presence filled this house.

A small bedroom on the top floor was occupied; a man and woman were asleep there. He closed the door gently, but didn't lock it.

There were two other doors on this landing, both locked. He took out a penknife with a pick-lock blade and started to work on one of them. At last the lock clicked back.

He groped for a light switch, pressed it down, and looked about a room twice as large as Ilott's, but almost identical; the layman could not tell the difference between one set of equipment and another. It was much less tidy than Ilott's; that was the only difference he saw.

No one was here.

Except for the couple asleep in the small room, the house was empty. Dawlish was disappointed, told himself he hadn't expected for a moment to find Kimble, and hurried down the stairs. It was after two; Terry might soon be back.

There was no sign of the youth, in the house or in the street. Dawlish drove off, with an empty feeling of frustration.

He drove to the Golden Shoe.

He wasn't surprised that the commissionaire let him pass without question; so did the sultry-looking girl who had tried to save Tim Jeremy from the strong-arm men. She even said, "Hallo Mr. Dawlish." He nodded and went up, hearing music from the main room. He wasn't interested in music, tried another door, opened it, and saw Carlotta at a table with a type-writer in front of her. She started up.

"Mr. Daw—" she cut the name short, and stood up.

"Hallo," said Dawlish in his normal speaking voice. "Is the great man in?"

"Mr. Mascatti is, but . . ." She hesitated as he drew near, and whispered:

"*Rutter back?*"

She nodded.

"*Hear them?*" Dawlish raised his voice. "Ask him if he can spare me a few minutes, will you?"

"Yes, Mr. Dawlish. *Yes, but it wasn't anything important.*"

"Thanks. *Ilott mentioned?*"

"*No.*" She sat down again and picked up a telephone, turned a handle, and waited. "Excuse me, Mr. Mascatti, but Mr. Dawlish is here and would like you to spare him a few minutes." She paused. "Yes, I'll tell him, thank you." She rang off, and said in a normal speaking voice: "He says he's engaged for the next ten minutes but will see you after that. Can you wait?"

Dawlish looked round, saw an upright chair, and pulled it nearer the desk.

"Yes. *Think we're overheard?*"

"*It wouldn't surprise me.*"

"*Keep your ears open for anything to do with Dr. Ilott.* Nice office you have here," he went on loudly. "I wonder if there could be such a thing as a drink."

"I think it could be arranged," said Carlotta. She rang a bell and a waiter came in. "Whisky-and-soda?"

"Please."

"At once, Maurice," said Carlotta. She was completely self-possessed here and was obviously used to being obeyed for the man went off at once. The girl sat at the typewriter with the same air of repressed vitality, and her lovely eyes were full of questions.

Dawlish whispered, "*What time do you finish?*"

"*Any time now.*"

"*Wait for me at Piccadilly Circus—near Swan and Edgars.*"

Maurice brought in the whisky-and-soda.

"Ah, thanks," said Dawlish. "The later it is the thirstier I get! They have good whisky here; I remember that from last night."

She started to type; she was a good typist, and hardly looked away from her notes. He remembered her story and marvelled that her English was so good that she could work on it as if it were her native language. There were puzzling things about Carlotta; about Terry Kimble; about Dr. Ilott.

A bell rang.

Carlotta started.

"You can go in now," she said, and stood up to lead Dawlish towards the door. She opened it, as Mascatti rose from his big desk. There was an armchair in front of the desk, ready for Dawlish. There was another armchair; Sir Anthony Kimble leaned back in it, apparently fast asleep.

CHAPTER XIX

KIMBLE SLEEPS

Kimble looked completely at rest, yet sleep had not ironed out the deep lines of anxiety at his lips. He was a nice-looking old boy, with a fringe of wispy white hair, a large pink bald patch, full lips, pursed as he breathed. He wasn't plump, and his clothes were a little too large for him; his stiff butterfly collar was much too large. He wore a cravat fastened by a gold ring, a dark grey suit, and lace-up boots.

Mascatti joined Dawlish.

"He came to see me two hours or so ago," he said. "He told me he had found the papers he thought I had stolen, and wanted to make it up. Of course, I agreed. He was so tired that I made him comfortable in this chair. I don't think he will easily be disturbed, do you? He looked completely exhausted when he arrived."

"Yes," said Dawlish. "Tired. Did you expect him?"

"No." Mascatti sat down. Dawlish noticed his perfectly white and well-kept hands. Mascatti was too handsome and too smooth to be true, yet Dawlish found himself doubting his own suspicions.

"So I shall not need your help with him," Mascatti said.

"Pity."

"But you can do something else for me, Mr. Dawlish."

"Before we go any further," Dawlish said, "what was the bone of contention?"

Mascatti placed the tips of his fingers together. "There's no reason why you shouldn't be told. You know me as a restaurateur and a business man, but I have other interests—humanitarian interests. Some years ago I asked Kimble to do some research work for me, into the causes and cure of several obscure diseases very prevalent in Italy—my native country—and liable to become endemic in crowded, insanitary conditions. Kimble prepared a long report and produced a drug to alleviate. Between the time I asked him to do the work and the completion of it, conditions changed in several parts of the world. The disease, little known outside Italy, occurred with dangerous frequency in various parts of the Middle and Far East, even in Germany during the summer. Kimble's treatment, the drug treatment, was more effective than any other known. Consequently it became valuable. The formula was lost during the time that Kimble and I were discussing terms. He is not a business man and did not appear to be interested in handling the commercial side of the drug, but he wanted payment which I thought was exorbitant. Understand, won't you, that the drug will be expensive to make commercially and at present there are practically no supplies."

Mascatti paused. Dawlish could almost imagine himself in a Harley Street consulting-room, listening to a great panjandrum of the medical world.

"Kimble asked for a large outright sum," Mascatti said. "I was prepared to give him a small sum in advance of a share in profits. Neither of us wanted large profits, but considerable capital was required to manufacture on a big scale. We agreed on one point—it was better to manufacture privately than to leave it to one of the great drug houses, with which the commercial aspect would be predominant, or at least would be over-emphasized. Moreover, before one of them could begin manufacture they would need months if not years to make their own tests and preparations. This drug is needed urgently for use in all places where displaced persons are living in dreadful conditions. India and Pakistan, for instance, are scourged by the disease."

"I see," said Dawlish, and found this more unreal than ever, yet strangely convincing.

"The formula was lodged with me," said Mascatti, "and I paid a reasonable sum in advance—one thousand pounds. Then the formula was lost, from my desk here. It happened on a day when Kimble had been in, wanting more money, and when I had left him in the office alone for some time. It was a trying day. I came in and put all my papers in the safe, afterwards, without checking that all of them were present. Next day I missed the formula. We accused each other. Kimble was hysterical with distress, and we almost came to blows. Regrettable, but . . ." He shrugged.

"No copy?" asked Dawlish.

"Kimble is a most impracticable man, and I'd had no time to have one made. It had to be done by a specialist, of course; I couldn't do it myself or simply hand it to a secretary. Well!" Mascatti became brisk. "This happened a little over a month ago. During the past month I've learned that Kimble is in very great need of money—I don't know why. Probably he is being blackmailed, as he told you. I thought he was consulting you over the loss of the formula, whereas it is more likely he wanted to see you about his other difficulties. You can see how the misunderstanding arose, can't you?"

"Just about," agreed Dawlish. "I don't see how you got the formula back and how you can be sure it wasn't copied."

Mascatti chuckled.

"Kimble had it all the time—he'd put it in his pocket and it had slipped through a torn lining, so he told me. He said that he was so tired that he must rest. He dropped off quickly. Now that I've been frank with you, will you be frank with me?" added Mascatti. "Were you drunk last night?"

"No."

"You acted very well, Mr. Dawlish."

"Thanks," said Dawlish dryly. "This all sounds remarkable. Kimble just walked in, did he?"

"Yes."

"Did he say where he had been?"

"No. Hasn't he been at home?"

"Not for some time," said Dawlish. "He was almost listed as missing."

"He's been very worried," said Mascatti. "I would like to help him. I'd like to find out if he is being blackmailed, and if so, by whom. That's the work I'd want you to do for me."

Dawlish gulped. "For *you*."

"Yes. And incidentally for him, of course."

"Yes, indeed," said Dawlish. "I'll help."

"I thought you would."

"And start right here. What do you know about your manager—Rutter?"

Mascatti actually laughed.

"Rutter is one of the most thorough-going scoundrels I know, but good at his job and, I believe, faithful to me. I find him very useful. He has contacts in the less salubrious parts of London, and I am not always interested in the letter of the law."

"Oh," said Dawlish. "I see." Was Mascatti so naïve as he pretended? Dawlish lit a cigarette, feeling that he needed a drink. "And now all I have to do is find out who is blackmailing Kimble. Mind if I take him home?"

"With you?" Mascatti looked surprised.

"Oh, no. His own home."

"I think it's a pity to wake him," said Mascatti. "I shall be here for another two hours, and if necessary I can sleep on the premises. He's quite safe here. I think you ought to leave him."

Dawlish rubbed his broken nose with the tip of his left forefinger and said:

"Perhaps you're right. Mind if I stay?"

"Why?"

"I'd like to be around when he wakes."

"Please yourself," said Mascatti, "but I must get you a more comfortable chair." He stretched his hand out for the bell-push and drew it back sharply, snapped his fingers as if in exasperation, stood up, and went to the door leading to Carlotta's office. As he went he muttered, "I should have sent that child home a long time ago." He pulled open the door. "Ah, Miss Morlay, I'd forgotten you were still here. I'm sorry I've kept you so late. Tell the doorman to get you a taxi and then have another armchair brought into my office, will you?"

"Yes, Mr. Mascatti."

"And if I keep you so late again, keep reminding me that you're here!" said Mascatti genially.

Dawlish, just behind him, shook his head at Carlotta, and hoped she realized that it meant that their appointment was cancelled. Mascatti gave him a chance to make it clear, for the telephone bell rang and he hurried to answer it. Dawlish had two minutes alone with Carlotta.

"Go straight home," he said.

"I think I'd better. Why are you staying?"

"There's more to do."

Her eyes searched his, and although the pupils were enlarged and she was obviously tired the burning intensity was still there.

"Is everything all right?"

"It will be."

"I hope you mean that," she said, and although she didn't put it into words she meant that she hoped she could trust him. She lifted another telephone. Mascatti was still talking in his office. She waited, frowning.

"Why is that doorman so long?" She tapped her foot on the floor with impatience. "Usually he is quicker. I will go and see—" She jumped up and hurried across the room.

Dawlish stood alone, listening to Mascatti, who sounded excited. Dawlish felt as if he had been turned upside down and had the sense shaken out of him. None of this squared with what he had taken for granted.

"No!" shouted Mascatti. "I cannot believe it! I will come as soon as I can—yes, early in the morning. Now!" He banged down the receiver, swung round, and almost ran to Dawlish. "Mr. Dawlish, a fantastic thing has happened. One of my restaurants, the one in Birmingham, has been held up. Over a hundred people were robbed. Many of them are ill, I understand. It's disastrous. Please take Kimble away. I must leave, and I don't want him here alone. I—"

The door through which Carlotta had gone burst open. She slammed it behind her and came rushing across the room, face chalk-white.

"Be careful!" She almost choked. "There are men outside, armed men, I—"

Dawlish bounded towards the door but didn't reach it before

it opened. Two men strode in, both masked, both armed. Mascatti uttered a groaning sound, Carlotta stifled a scream.

"Just keep quiet and you'll be all right." The first man's muffled voice came from behind his mask. "Where's the safe?"

CHAPTER XX

KIMBLE WAKES

"You heard me," the man repeated roughly. "Where's the safe? You can give me the keys and tell me where it is, Mascatti, that'll save you time and trouble, too."

"You can't—" began Carlotta wildly.

The second man went across and slapped her face. Mascatti stood quite still, as if afraid to move. Dawlish was too near the other door; a mistake. A gun was trained on his stomach. Carlotta, face red with the fingermarks, leaned helplessly against the desk.

"Okay, take it the hard way," said the first man, and stepped towards Mascatti, pushing the gun into his stomach. He struck Mascatti on the face with his free hand. "Talk, quick."

Mascatti didn't speak—but kicked. Dawlish hadn't expected him to have the courage. He caught the gunman on the shin. The man gasped and staggered away—and fired. The roar of the shot was deafening, but Mascatti didn't move. The other gunman rushed forward, lured to a mistake—he didn't watch Dawlish.

Dawlish hit him, felt his neck give and saw him thud to the

floor. Mascatti stood quite still, Carlotta stood with her hands raised towards the ceiling. Dawlish bent down, snatched the gun which his man had dropped, and saw the first gunman swinging towards them.

They fired.

Dawlish felt nothing as the shots roared out simultaneously. The gunman staggered, and his right arm dropped. Dawlish didn't fire again, just leapt and sent him flying with a left hook. The man's arms waved wildly. Carlotta jumped forward, plucked at his gun, which was nearly out of his grasp, got it, and backed away.

"In there." Dawlish pointed to the inner door. "Don't argue." He went to the outer door, which was ajar—but it closed before he reached it. He saw a movement outside, fired, but didn't know whether he'd scored a hit. He pulled at the door; it didn't open.

He pulled again; it wouldn't budge.

Mascatti said: "They've locked it. I—Dawlish! The other room!"

He turned and ran, reaching his own office a yard in front of Dawlish. Dawlish passed him, saw a masked gunman at the other door, peering round. Two shots rang out. Dawlish felt a bullet pluck at his sleeve and a sharp twinge of pain. The other man bent at the knees and wobbled—but as he fell the door behind him closed.

The echoes of the shooting died.

Dawlish went slowly to the other door and tried the handle, but it wouldn't move. Mascatti and Carlotta stood close together in the doorway between the rooms.

Through it all Kimble slept.

Dawlish went across to the cupboard where he knew Mascatti kept his drinks, took out a bottle of cognac, poured a little into two glasses and took them across to Mascatti and the girl. Dawlish poured himself out a whisky and said:

"Better sit down."

He didn't wait to see whether they obeyed but went into Carlotta's office. One of the men was still unconscious, the other was trying to sit up. Dawlish yanked him to his feet and sat him in Carlotta's chair, then bent over the other man, using the victim's own tie to fasten his hands behind his back. Then he tied the man's shoe-laces together. He turned to the man in the chair.

"Get up."

The man obeyed.

"Other room."

Dawlish walked behind him as he went unsteadily. Mascatti and Carlotta were sitting down; the only colour they boasted between them was the red imprint of the man's hand on Carlotta's cheek.

The man whom Dawlish had shot lay still, with blood oozing from his chest. Dawlish went across to him, knelt down on one knee, and looked at his face and felt his pulse. The man was dead.

Dawlish straightened up.

Mascatti said, "We—we're locked in."

"That's right," said Dawlish. "Electric control?"

"Yes. I have valuables in my safe and take all precautions. The—the control switch is outside."

"Pity. Not that you can complain, Nick." Dawlish grinned. "If you hadn't taken the chance of a bullet where it would hurt, we'd be worse off. Were you hurt?"

"No—no, not even scratched. But—what can we do?"

Dawlish lifted the telephone, paused, and put it down.

"The line's dead. We'll have to possess ourselves in patience."

"But outside—in the club—" Mascatti threw up his hands, was more continental than Dawlish had seen him. "What is happening? What *is* happening? First Birmingham, now—"

"It'll work out," said Dawlish. "We can't do anything in time to stop any raid. A nice inside job."

"*Inside* job?"

Dawlish looked at him thoughtfully and said: "You'd better have another spot of brandy. You need it. Take it easy, Carlotta."

Carlotta, looking much better, stood up and went across to Kimble and stared down, as if she couldn't believe that he was really there. Dawlish lit a cigarette, gave a gun to Mascatti, and said:

"Watch him, won't you?" He nodded to the conscious prisoner then went to the door of the outer room and tried it again. There wasn't any chance of opening it—not only was it electrically controlled, but it was made of steel; he heard the faint ring as he tapped it with his knuckles. He tried the other door and Mascatti, sitting at the desk and looking uncomfortable with the gun in his hand, said unsteadily:

"You can do nothing about it, Dawlish. I made quite sure of that."

"How thick is the wall?"

"Twelve inches."

"Quite a strong-room."

"It was meant to be," said Mascatti.

"Not a bad job, all round." Dawlish went across to the prisoner, who was leaning drunkenly against the wall, and said in a light, conversational tone:

"Who's behind this?"

The man muttered, "I don't know." He was big and looked ugly. He had little eyes and a low forehead and a huge chin, with a gash for a mouth and a nose with practically no bridge. "I—I don't know."

Dawlish said: "You know all right. I'll break your bones one by one until you tell me. Who's behind it?"

The man seemed to try to press himself through the wall to get away from Dawlish. The others watched, tensely. Dawlish raised his right hand, took the man's wrist, and began to twist; and he meant to hurt.

The man screamed.

"Who is it?" Dawlish growled.

Sweat stood out in little beads on the other's forehead, lined his upper lip, made his collar damp.

"It—it's Rutter! Rutter, he—"

Mascatti said, "No." His voice sounded strangled, hardly seemed to come from him. "No," he repeated, "it can't be."

"Is Rutter downstairs?" demanded Dawlish.

"Yes, he led the raid; he—"

"What's he going to do?"

"Hold up everyone, rob them. We had to clear out the safe."

Dawlish released him; he fell against the wall and slithered down, nearly to the floor. He had to struggle to get to a standing position again, and looked weak and pain-wracked. Dawlish turned his back on him. There wasn't much more to fear from him, danger only threatened from outside. He wouldn't let himself think of what might be happening there—at the mews flat, for instance. At least Beresford was with Felicity.

Mascatti sat at the desk with his hands spread out on it.

"Rutter," he said in a low voice. "So Rutter turned on me."

"It looks like it," said Dawlish with unaccustomed gentleness. "Anyone who trusted Rutter was asking for trouble."

"Do you think Rutter was blackmailing Kimble?"

"I'm pretty sure he was."

"Rutter," breathed Mascatti. "If I can once get my hands on him—"

"The danger is that he might get his hands on us," said Dawlish dryly. "If he wants the safe badly enough." He went across to the communicating door and swung it. "Pretty heavy. Is this electrically controlled, too?"

"No."

"Have you the only key, or has Rutter one?"

"Rutter has one. I don't understand—"

"We'll barricade this door and your outer one, and leave Miss Morlay's room empty," said Dawlish. "Desk and chairs against that door, her furniture against this. I don't think we ought to lose much time." He spoke casually, trying not to add to Mascatti's nervous tension. "You bring the light stuff in, will you, Carlotta?"

She hurried into her office.

Dawlish and Mascatti carried her desk and two filing cabinets in, and when the door was closed pushed them against it. Mascatti strained and heaved and sweated, Dawlish made it seem easy. He placed the furniture so that it would be hard to shift from outside, then moved the bigger furniture of Mascatti's office against the steel door. It was twenty minutes before they had finished, and Mascatti was pale and trembling with nervous strain and physical exertion.

Carlotta pushed the hair back from her forehead.

"What now?" she asked.

"We just wait," said Dawlish. Nothing in his manner hinted at his tearing anxiety to get out, to make sure that Felicity was safe. "I expect Rutter—"

He broke off, catching sight of a movement out of the corners of his eyes. It came from Kimble. Kimble drew up his legs, and yawned, then blinked. All three stared at him. Carlotta stepped towards him, but Dawlish held her back. Kimble yawned again, rubbed his eyes, and sat up. He blinked round at them. He looked rather absurd, pink and white and helpless. There was a pathetic touch about him, and something else. Kimble wasn't worldly. Even when he caught sight of them all, and started, he didn't react like an ordinary human being. The furniture piled at the doors seemed to mean nothing to him.

He put his hands on the arms of his chair, stood up, stifled a yawn, and said:

"Dear me. I must have dropped off. Why, Carlotta, my dear! How nice to see you again. And Mr. Mascatti—why, of course." He beamed; no one could have looked more delighted. "Of *course*. You were good enough to let me rest here, weren't you. It must be getting late. Oughtn't you to go home, Carlotta?"

He was too fatherly to be true.

"Soon," said Carlotta, with a catch in her voice. "As soon as—"

The telephone bell rang. It startled Mascatti, who swung round towards it; it stood on a chair, one of the few pieces of furniture which had been saved from the barricades. He snatched it up, dropped it, snatched and exclaimed:

"We're connected again!"

Dawlish didn't speak. Kimble looked puzzled—and licked his lips, as a thirsty man might.

"Hallo!" cried Mascatti.

"It's the house-telephone," Carlotta said.

Mascatti's excitement died, hope faded, his knuckles showed white where he gripped the other receiver. Even Kimble was caught up in the tension.

CHAPTER XXI

DEMAND

There was only one house-telephone.

Dawlish went to Mascatti's side and could hear a faint sound, perhaps of Rutter's voice. Mascatti was pressing his hand against his forehead and his eyes were glassy. He kept licking his lips.

He muttered: "No. No, I won't do it. No."

He listened.

"What won't you do?" demanded Dawlish.

"I won't do it," said Mascatti into the telephone. "I won't bargain."

Dawlish took the telephone from his fingers; he didn't put up much of a struggle, just backed a pace and stared at Dawlish; his face was like a death's head.

"Rutter?" Dawlish asked quietly.

"Well, well, well!" sneered Rutter. "If it isn't the great Dawlish himself. How do you like it when you're on the losing side, Dawlish?"

"I'm used to it."

"So you are!" Rutter's voice was shrill with excitement. "You'll get more used to it. Listen—I want Kimble. I've told Old Nick."

He made a sound that was more giggle than laugh. "Fooled you about Old Nick, didn't I? Now listen. I want Kimble. I'm going to open the door in five minutes' time, and Kimble's to come out on his own. If anyone else shows up they'll be shot. And if no one shows up, I'll spray gas into the room. Understand? Just send Kimble out. Don't worry about Old Nick's tender heart, just make him do what I want. Or else . . ." He made a noise in his throat; an imitation death rattle.

He rang off.

Mascatti said hoarsely, "Did he tell you?"

"Please, I don't want to be difficult but I must understand what is happening." Kimble raised a hand, palm outwards, as if he were in a pulpit. "Why are all these things piled up at the doors? What is happening here? I *must* be told."

"We're—locked in," Carlotta said weakly.

"Locked in? I still don't understand."

Dawlish said: "It's easy. The club's been raided, there are thieves outside, and they want to get in. We're keeping them out."

Kimble backed to a chair, dropped on to the arm, and said, "Oh, dear." He sounded like an old maid. "Oh, dear," he repeated. "Who is—it's *Rutter*! That man! I heard you name him, so I'm right. Aren't I?"

"Yes."

A voice broke off across the word, deep, in a way unnatural, undoubtedly Rutter's. It came from a box on the desk by the door—the internal broadcasting system had been left on.

"The door's open. Remember what I said, Dawlish. Either Kimble comes out or I'll kill the lot of you. I'll send you to sleep, and you won't wake up."

He stopped.

Carlotta closed her eyes, Mascatti leaned heavily against

a chair and watched the box. Dawlish was only interested in Kimble. The threat did something to the old man. He seemed to shrink, his knees bent, he took one step towards a chair, so that he could lean against it. His hands were stretched out beseechingly.

"Get moving!" Rutter ordered.

"No," whispered Kimble. "No, he can't know. He *can't* know." He pressed his hands against his eyes, as if to shut out a nightmare vision. There was silence, and all three of them watched, touched by the horror which was in him. Gradually he stood up, threw out his chest with a conscious effort and stepped towards the outer door.

"Move that furniture, please."

"Dr. Kimble!" cried Carlotta.

"No." Mascatti moved towards him and touched his arm. "We can't allow—"

"Don't be silly," said Kimble, and turned to Dawlish. "Mr. Dawlish, I hope you have some sense. The ultimatum is quite final, and I must accept it. Otherwise he will carry out his threat. I didn't think he had discovered—" He broke off.

Dawlish asked mildly, "Discovered what?"

"I suppose you had better know," said Kimble. "I made a discovery during the course of my researches. I left a copy of my notes in my wallet; I hoped you'd find it. Obviously Rutter did, when he came and took me away. I was seeking a synthetic plasma. In the course of experimenting I found a serum which, when administered in small doses, acts as a narcotic. It can be made gaseous, and kept in airproof phials, or used as a powder or a liquid. It is tasteless and has no smell. In large doses it kills. One sleeps—and dies. And if Rutter has it he will use it on you. I can't have that on my conscience. Please move the furniture."

Rutter's voice crackled into the room.

"I won't wait much longer."

Dawlish glanced at the steel door. In two minutes he could pull away some of the furniture, and Kimble could walk through, as Kimble wanted to. Carlotta moved towards it and stood facing them, as if prepared to prevent him from moving the furniture with her life; it didn't look as if she were striking a pose.

"They can't kill us as easily as that," Mascatti said hoarsely.

"Any ventilation slots?" asked Dawlish.

"Yes, but—"

"Then of course they can do it. They can pass gas through the slots, and we shall have no chance of defending ourselves," said Kimble. "I don't understand these heroics, especially from a man of your character, Mr. Dawlish. Either way, I shall be in danger. Out there I shall have a chance to live; in here, none."

"They won't kill. They're bluffing." Mascatti was pulling at his hair.

"You don't know Rutter, even though he works for you," Kimble said. The man acted as if he wanted to go out; the thought hit Dawlish and lingered. Would it ever be possible to explain Kimble's behaviour? "Let's waste no more time."

"Send Kimble out!" Rutter demanded through the loud-speaker. "I won't wait any longer. Send him out."

"At once," Kimble said.

"How much of this stuff have they?" asked Dawlish.

"I don't know—don't ask silly questions." Kimble was impa-tient; as impatient as Rutter. He moved towards the door, stood for a moment in front of Carlotta, smiled, and placed his hands on her shoulders. "You're very sweet. I wish I had been able to help you more. Perhaps I shall be able to, in future." He took his hand away and pulled at a chair. He leaned towards the speaking-box, and said, "I'm coming, Rutter, be a little patient."

"*Hurry.*"

"Dawlish, please help," said Kimble.

Dawlish went across and began to move the heavy chairs. Carlotta looked as if she would throw herself at him bodily. She actually moved forward, but Kimble's glance stopped her. Dawlish heaved at the big desk, had it a foot away from the door, saw Kimble move forward, and heard Mascatti cry:

"Stop!"

Mascatti was standing half the room away, with one of the captured guns in his hand.

"Come away, Dawlish. Rutter can do his damndest, but *I* won't help."

Dawlish straightened up from the table. With Tim and Ted here, he could have done a lot; on his own, with the crosscurrents and the antagonism and the menace, there was little he could do without relying on luck; and he needed much more than he could expect. If he told Mascatti what he intended to do, Kimble would hear; and Kimble would make difficulties. Carlotta still looked as if she would fling herself bodily at him. He pushed his fingers through his hair, as Kimble said:

"Ignore him!"

"You can't ignore a pistol," Dawlish said. It wasn't really warm in here, but he was sweating. He approached Kimble, hands by his sides—and as he drew up in front of the man he snatched one hand out of his pocket and cracked an uppercut to the chin. Kimble gasped. Dawlish stopped him from falling, and didn't need to hit him again. He lifted him and carried him across to the chair where he had slept.

Carlotta and Mascatti hurried across.

"What—" began the girl.

"Quiet," said Dawlish, and whispered: "I'm going out."

Understanding dawned in Mascatti's eyes. Carlotta turned and looked at Kimble.

Dawlish said, "Don't take any notice of what I'm going to say." He paused and raised his voice. "Mascatti! Get away from there. Kimble's going. *Shut up!*" He roared the words. "I'm not going to let myself be killed for an old fool of a man. Get out of my way!" He picked up a small chair and hurled it across the room. It crashed; Rutter must have heard a noise. Dawlish went across to the furniture and pulled the desk further away. Then he stood close to the door, and beckoned the others. Carlotta reached him first and pulled at the door; it didn't start to move until Mascatti helped her.

It moved slowly. Dawlish couldn't see outside. He flattened himself against the wall until the door was open enough for him to get through. Then he lowered himself almost to his knees, crouching. He took a gun from his right-hand pocket, used his left hand to support himself against the floor.

"Kimble! Hurry!" He snapped the words.

No one spoke outside.

Dawlish snarled, "Hurry, you little squirt!"

Then he went forward, still crouching. He saw a shadowy figure in the doorway, and fired. The figure disappeared. He heard a shout. A shot roared out from the passage, but he was outside now. The bullet smacked against the steel door.

The light went on, vivid, blinding. He narrowed his eyes and fired twice, hit the lamp, and plunged the passage into darkness. He heard stealthy movements, thought he heard the hiss of gas. Rutter might be able to do exactly what he said. Dawlish fired, blindly. Someone shouted. He fired in the direction of the cry, and heard a thud, as of a body falling. He expected a fusillade to come towards him, and shifted his position, standing upright

149

now. Two bullets smacked into the wall, only inches away from him.

With luck, the shooting would be heard from outside.

With luck. . . .

He heard nothing, and the silence was uncanny. Silence? Was the hissing sound real, or imaginary—like the soft hiss of gas from an open tap. He fired again and jumped to one side, but there was no answering shout. Just silence. He wished the light would come on now, he'd take a chance if only he could see.

He felt a strange lassitude. It didn't creep up on him; he was suddenly tired. He yawned. Then panic clutched and stimulated him to action. He shouted and fired twice. The flashes of the shots showed a landing empty except for one man who lay on his face, curiously huddled. He thought he heard shouting from a long way off—but it might be near, he might not be hearing properly.

He yawned again.

He felt himself staggering, wanted only to lie down, to rest.

Even panic was lost in that all-enveloping weariness.

CHAPTER XXII

SLEEP

Ted Beresford sat in the big armchair at the flat and spoke into the telephone. Tim Jeremy stood watching him, red-eyed, but no longer morose; he was worried. Cigarette butts littered three ash-trays, empty tankards were near. It was nearly half past three, and they had been together in the living-room for several hours.

Felicity was still sleeping.

Beresford said, "Sorry, Mrs. Trivett, I know you've been asleep, but is Bill there?"

He listened.

"All right, thanks," he said. "I'll try again." He rang off, and shook his head. "Bill's at the Yard or out on a job, he was called out half an hour ago. Better try the Yard again, I suppose, but the beggars won't give me any information." He began to dial. "I wouldn't have minded so much if Pat had telephoned before twelve."

Tim said, "Ilott says he didn't leave until after twelve."

Beresford shrugged, then spoke briskly, "Yes, you can help me—Superintendent Trivett, please." He lifted his head sharply.

"Yes, I would!" He glanced eagerly at Jeremy. "He's just got back, I—hallo. Hallo, Bill, this is Ted Beresford. I want—"

Trivett obviously cut him short. Jeremy drew nearer, hands clenched. Beresford caught his breath, but didn't speak. He seemed to listen for a long time; then:

"All right. Yes, I heard you. Thanks."

He put down the receiver slowly, and Jeremy started to speak and stopped himself. Beresford cleared his throat before he said:

"Pat's—sleeping."

Jeremy didn't speak.

"Trouble at the Golden Shoe. Mascatti and Carlotta are sleeping, too. And—" He jumped up. "What are we standing here for? Let's go there."

"Can't." Jeremy was abrupt.

"Why—oh, Fel. Yes, of course. Can't both leave her. I—"

The front-door bell rang. He turned with surprising agility on his false leg, and hurried along the passage, with Tim close behind him, but he didn't open the door immediately. He stood to one side, and put his right hand into his pocket, the fingers closing about his gun. As he did so, there was an unexpected call from outside; the hoot of an owl.

He started. "Who—"

"That'll be Roger!" Tim opened the door, making a fair imitation of the hoot of an owl—an identifying signal Dawlish and his friends had often used.

It was Brent, who came in quickly.

"Just come from the Golden Shoe," he said abruptly. "I've been watching for Carlotta. Two or three men arrived there an hour ago, and there was shooting. That didn't start until a little while before I left." He was speaking jerkily, as if he had been running. "I tried to get in, there were a couple of gunmen stopping anyone with that idea. Sent for the police. Pat's—" He didn't finish.

Beresford said: "Trivett just told us. We're going over. Will you stay outside Felicity's door?"

"Er—yes," said Brent. He was the youngest of the three, but looked tired, and what he had seen had sickened him. "Yes, all right. You won't find it good."

Beresford glared. There was silence—a taut silence, broken only by their breathing. Bleakness hardened the eyes of both Beresford and Jeremy. It was as if all three were afraid to speak again.

Beresford barked: "He's asleep. It's no worse, is it?"

"Not yet," Brent said.

Half a dozen police cars were outside the Golden Shoe, with two ambulances. A crowd of thirty or forty people had gathered, including several newspapermen who were nagging at the two uniformed policemen on duty to tell them what had happened. The policemen wouldn't speak. Other police were surrounding the club, moving the crowd on; or trying to. Beresford and Jeremy reached the door.

"Mr. Trivett's expecting us," Beresford said.

"Name, sir, please?"

"I'm Beresford."

"That's all right, sir."

"Oi, Beresford!" One of the newspapermen pushed closer. "Is Pat Dawlish in there?"

Beresford shrugged. "I shouldn't be surprised."

"What's it all about? Let's have a whisper."

"Sorry."

"We can run Dawlish, anyhow," one of the newspapermen said. "Might find out what he's up to, and work the story up from that."

Beresford and Jeremy went into the small hall. A policeman

stood against the cloak-room counter, and the sultry-looking girl sat on her chair—asleep. She was completely relaxed, her sultriness had gone, she looked pretty. The two men hurried up the stairs, Beresford ahead. At the first landing a man appeared from the club itself. There was no music, not a sound of any kind except the distant murmuring of voices.

The man was Dayson, one of Trivett's sergeants.

"Oh, hallo," he said grimly. "Come in."

They passed him.

The lights were full on. The room looked bright and gay. The revellers wore paper hats, streamers strewed the dance floor. Even the members of the band wore paper hats. The tables were dotted with champagne glasses and the usual oddments. Champagne bottles stood in silvered buckets on their little stands, but except for that distant murmur of voices there wasn't a sound.

Everyone here was asleep.

Beresford's gaze roamed the room. Every table seemed to be full. Men, women, dressed in their finery, leaned back on their chairs or forward on the tables—sleeping. Some of the women looked haggard. It was a hideous sight; and frightening.

Beresford jerked his head up.

In a corner two men and two women sat together. One of the men had a dark beard and moustache, and the scarlet paper hat perched on the back of his head made him look almost sinister—yet asleep.

Jeremy snapped, "Gertie!"

"And that's Ilott," Beresford said. "Who's that with—" He didn't need to go on, for the other man at that table was Terry Kimble. Gertie sat between them, another woman had her back to the door.

The mutter of voices went on and on.

Beresford said, "Where's Dawlish?"

Dayson pointed, but put a hand on his arm. "Recognize any of these people?"

"I should look after that bunch in the corner," said Beresford. "The bearded chap and the others." He turned slowly out of the room and made his way up the stairs and through the door, which stood ajar. This was an office, and the furniture was all at one end, near the door. A policeman stood in the middle of the room. The voices came from the adjoining room, and Beresford reached the communicating door first. He saw Trivett and two other Yard men—and Dawlish.

Dawlish was stretched out on the floor. He might be sleeping; he might also be dead. Beresford muttered under his breath, and went across. Until then, he hadn't seen Carlotta, sleeping in a chair, or Mascatti, perched on an upright chair and leaning back, looking uncomfortable—or the dead man.

A middle-aged man was bending over the girl, and straightened up as Beresford reached Dawlish.

"Well, I can't find anything," he said testily. "She's asleep, and that's all there is to it. Like the others."

Beresford saw that Dawlish was breathing.

"Better get them to hospital," the man said; he was a police-surgeon. "Not that you can do anything more than keep them under observation. Hell of a business."

"We'd better get them away," said Trivett. He stood near Dawlish, looking tired and red-eyed, but forced a smile when he saw Beresford and Jeremy. "Hallo, there. I don't think it's too bad, no sign of anything except sleeping beauties. Did you know Pat was coming here?"

"No." Beresford found himself looking at the girl whom he had first seen at Victoria Station. Even asleep, her character showed. "I—"

He stopped abruptly.

The girl stirred—the first movement that many of the sleeping people had made. Trivett saw it, too, and swung round; the police-surgeon bent down again.

"Don't crowd her!" he snapped.

Trivett and Beresford moved back.

She stirred again, moving her arm from one side to the other, yawned slightly, and her eyelids flickered. Then she settled down again. The others watched with fascinated attention. Then Trivett moved, as if he had given up hope that she was coming round. As he did so she gave a deep yawn and moved from one side of the chair to the other; and her eyelids flickered again.

She moved her lips.

"Miss Morlay." Trivett spoke gently. "Miss Morlay, don't go to sleep again. I'm a police officer, you're quite safe. Wake up."

She heard, for she stiffened, opened her eyes and blinked up. She closed her eyes again. The doctor took her shoulder and pressed gently. She tried to shrug herself free, but his grip tightened, and reluctantly she opened her eyes wide.

"Yes?" Her voice was only just audible.

"Take it easy," said Trivett, "but as soon as you can, I want you to tell me what happened."

"Happened?" she said, and struggled to an upright position. She was puzzled by the ring of men she didn't know. Then she saw Dawlish on the floor, and her hand sprang to her lips, stifling a shout. She jumped up, and her knees gave way. The doctor grabbed and saved her from falling, but she seemed oblivious, just stared round—at Mascatti and the policemen, back to Dawlish, then about the room.

"Where—is he?"

"Who?" Trivett kept his voice calm and normal.

"Dr. Kimble. Where—" She broke off, held her breath and then demanded in a shrill voice: "Is he here? Have you seen him?"

"No," said Trivett. "Are you sure he was here?"

"Of course he was!" It wouldn't take much to make her hysterical, she was glaring about the room as if she couldn't believe the evidence of her own eyes. "He was here! Rutter got him, Rutter—"

Trivett said, "Take it easy, Miss Morlay, you won't help us if you shout." He nodded to one of the men and pointed to the open cocktail cabinet. The man went across and hesitated, then poured out brandy. As he brought it across to her, Trivett asked:

"Was Rutter here?"

"He did all this! He locked us in, then threatened to kill us if we didn't give Dr. Kimble up. Dawlish went out, there was shooting. Is—is Mr. Dawlish hurt?"

"Not badly. He's sleeping, like the rest of you. He'll be all right." Trivett took the brandy glass and handed it to the girl. "Take a sip of this, and sit back for a few minutes." He turned away, and started to give instructions to his men—find Rutter. One man hurried out. A telephone downstairs was connected, and the call went off: find Rutter. Carlotta sipped the drink slowly, and sat back in the chair more comfortably. She looked dazed now—as much with fear as from the physical effect of the sleep.

A shout came, from outside the room. A man spoke calmly, and there was another shout, then a crash. Trivett glared at the door. One of his men hurried across, but before he reached it, Ilott staggered into the room. Dayson was grabbing at his arm, uselessly, Ilott simply shrugged his hand off and came towards Trivett unsteadily. He looked ferocious. He let his gaze roam, and it fell upon Carlotta.

He stopped moving.

As he looked at her his expression changed, he gave a little choking cry and put out a hand as if to save himself from falling.

"Are you—all right?"

"Yes," she said. "Yes, I'm all right. What are—you doing here?" Her voice seemed to come from a long way off. "I thought you didn't like—night clubs."

He waved his hand.

"Doesn't matter. I wanted—no, it doesn't matter. So long as you're all right. Don't remember me, do you?"

"*Remember* you? Of course; I came to see you—"

"Oh, not then. Years ago. You were only a kid. I did some work with your father—Dr. Morlay. Yes, in Prague. Came to the house once, I remember . . ." He shook his head foolishly. "Didn't have a beard. Doesn't matter, provided you're all right. Sure you are?"

She managed to smile. "Thank you, yes. I—"

"Good. That's very good." Ilott turned and gave Trivett and Beresford a sickly grin. "I don't feel very well," he said. "Need a drink. Mind if—"

He didn't finish, for footsteps sounded in the doorway, and Terry Kimble came across unsteadily, saw Carlotta, broke into a little run towards her, then stopped halfway as if he knew he couldn't run without falling.

"You're here. Wonderful! I—where's Dad? Do you know? Where's Dad?"

CHAPTER XXIII

LOOT

No one answered him.

Trivett and his men watched the youngster closely, Ilott stared, and did not seem to be sympathetic. He wasn't wearing his glasses, and his gaze actually looked hostile. Beresford and Jeremy studied Terry's face, but it was left to Carlotta to say:

"He's not here, Terry. They took him away."

"Oh, no!" cried Terry. "Not . . ." He paused, swallowed words, and then went on thickly: "Not again. Not just after he'd been released. It's too cruel, it—"

Ilott snapped, "Why don't you behave like a man, even if—"

"Who the hell do you think you're talking to?" Terry shouted, and colour burned his cheeks. "I'll knock that sneer off your face if you talk to me like that again." He advanced threateningly; his red hair didn't bely him, he was always spoiling for a fight.

Carlotta's tone of voice altered.

"Don't be ridiculous, Terry. It isn't Dr. Ilott's fault."

"How did your father get free?" Ilott asked reluctantly, as if he knew that he should really show interest.

"I don't know. Simply know he was. He 'phoned me." Terry put a hand on Carlotta's arm. "Look here, it's time you were home. Madness to stay up any longer. Nothing you can do. I'll drive you home."

"I—" began Ilott, and stopped abruptly.

Trivett said, "I'd like to ask you a few questions before you go away, Mr. Kimble." He seemed to have given up thought of questioning Carlotta, even though Carlotta was much more calm and collected. "I'll send Miss Morlay home in one of our cars, and—"

"Nonsense. I'll take her in mine," said Ilott. He looked delighted at the opportunity, put a hand on Carlotta's arm, snatched it away again as if the gesture were an impertinence, and led the way to the outer door. No one tried to stop them, but Terry Kimble was obviously torn with rage.

Tim Jeremy followed; his Riley purred after the little Austin through the dark, quiet streets of the West End.

Half an hour later Dawlish came round.

He was among the first, but before dawn, everyone who had slept at the Golden Shoe was awake—except those who would never wake. There were three, sitting at the tables amid the scene of gaiety and glitter, with a peaceful look on their dead faces. A dozen little glass phials, all broken, were on the floor; the gas containers which had made this possible.

At half past seven Dawlish and Beresford reached the flat. Roger Brent had heard the car, and was at the door to greet them. Telephone messages had reassured Dawlish about Felicity and kept Brent abreast of the news.

The sleep hadn't refreshed Dawlish for long, and the two-hour talk with Trivett had tired him out. His eyes were heavy and he felt sluggish. Yet he went into the bedroom and looked down at Felicity, forgot tiredness, forgot even the nagging sense of fear of what might happen next.

Trivett had that fear of tomorrow. He hadn't said so, but Dawlish knew that there wasn't a man at the Yard not touched by it. This didn't come within their usual scope, and they were still in the dark. Dawlish had told them what Kimble had said about his drug; how much Rutter had and where it would be used next.

Rutter hadn't been found.

Mascatti had come round, and was now at the Yard, being questioned—a sick, ill-looking Mascatti. He had reason to feel sick. Except that there had been no shooting, his Birmingham restaurant had been raided in the same way.

One factor would set the headlines of every newspaper screaming more shrilly. The pockets of all the guests had been emptied; not a piece of jewellery remained on finger, dress, throat—anywhere. Everyone at the Golden Shoe and at the other restaurant had been stripped of valuables.

Dawlish, knowing all that, yawned again, couldn't fight off the weariness, and went to bed.

He felt something touch his forehead gently. He stirred. He heard faint movements, and opened one eye. It was bright in the room, and the sun burnished Felicity's hair as she backed out of the door, looking towards him. She didn't know that he was watching her through his lashes. She went out, almost closed the door, and he said deeply:

"Stop, thief!"

She thrust the door open and hurried back.

"Brute! I thought you were asleep."

"Even I wake up, sometimes." Dawlish sat up, Felicity flung

herself on to the bed, kissed him, held his hands tightly and searched his face as if for tell-tale signs of injury. He noticed for the first time that his left arm was stiff. She moved the pyjamas sleeve, and he saw the bandage.

"A scratch," he said carelessly.

"*Are* you feeling all right?"

"Wonderful."

"Hungry?"

"Thirsty. What's the time?"

"Half past two."

"What?" cried Dawlish, and flung the bedclothes away. "Do you mean to say—"

She pushed his leg back into bed and pulled the clothes over him.

"Yes, I mean to say that it's half past two and there's no reason why you shouldn't relax for half an hour with the tea and papers. If you can relax with the papers. Nothing's happened since last night. I know what happened to me, now—I couldn't understand why I woke up fully dressed! Ted's been talking to Trivett, everything's as you were."

"Oh," said Dawlish.

Ten minutes later he was smoking, sipping tea and looking through the early editions of the evening papers. They had done the raid on the Golden Shoe full justice. There were photographs of him, Mascatti and of Carlotta Morlay. Some of Mascatti's gifts to medical research were mentioned. There wasn't a picture of Kimble, but the fact that Kimble had been kidnapped hit the headlines. The *Daily Echo* had the fullest story:

SLEEP DRUG KILLS THREE

RUTHLESS WAR ON KILLERS

Dawlish read, scowled, lit another cigarette, and studied the small paragraph in bold type, boxed on the front page, which told that Scotland Yard were anxious to interview Percival Rutter. There was no picture of Rutter either.

The telephone bell rang, by the bed. He lifted it, and heard Felicity say, "Mr. Dawlish isn't in."

"Felicity, I must talk to him." It was Trivett.

"Yes, Bill," said Dawlish.

Felicity banged down her receiver. Trivett asked polite questions, and then said: "What did you do with Percy Dipper? Ted's told me about that."

So the body had been found.

Dawlish said: "What do you know?"

"We've just found his body in Ilott's attic, with a surgeon's knife in the heart. But that didn't kill him. The drug did that—more sleepy death."

Dawlish talked. . . .

Ten minutes later when Dawlish was still trying to see Ilott as an accomplice of Rutter, the door opened and Felicity said: "Can you see Ted?"

"Of course I can see Ted."

"I suppose I'd better let you," said Felicity, "but I don't want you to overdo it today." Felicity was frightened, didn't want to show it, and covered it with a curiously naïve concern; a protecting, mothering Felicity.

"Darling," she said.

"Hm-hm?"

"You could leave it to Trivett, now."

"Oh, yes," said Dawlish, "and if I stay here long enough I will." He got out of bed and pulled on a dressing-gown as Ted appeared. "Mind telling me while I'm in the bath, Ted?"

"Glad to." Nothing was different about Beresford, even his dark hair was untidy, and his brown suit shapeless. He put an arm round Felicity's shoulder. "Don't worry about him, he has a lot of lives left."

Felicity sniffed.

In the bathroom Dawlish started to shave, while Beresford sat on the bathroom stool and talked. Dawlish finished shaving, had a shower; Beresford still talked. He had a photographic memory for conversations, and he told of what had happened at the Golden Shoe in minute detail. Dawlish seldom asked a question, then only to clarify a point. He went into the bedroom and dressed while Beresford finished.

"And that's it, Pat. The latest news is negative. No trace of Kimble or Rutter. Odd thing, but all photographs of Kimble have vanished. I sent 'em that snap found in the wallet, but the face is blurred, it won't be much good. His house was raided, and everything with a picture of Kimble in it was taken away. No one's ever seen a picture of Rutter. Police will probably dig something up. Well—what do you make of it?"

Felicity came in, with a meal that was an appetizing compromise between breakfast and lunch.

"Ah," said Dawlish appreciatively. "I must be all right, I can eat that and lashings more." Felicity put the tray down on the bedside table. "What's the matter with eating in the living-room?"

"We might get callers," said Felicity. "I don't want anyone to think we're living in a coffee shop"

"No, dear. Had any yet?"

"Carlotta Morlay called," said Felicity, "with that scarecrow of a man—what's his name? Ilott. He's fantastic. Terry Kimble came soon afterwards, and among the things he wanted to know was whether Carlotta had been here. I told him yes.

Would you believe it, I forgot to mention that Ilott had been with her! He hoped you would be all right and dashed off. To fight the world, I should think. And, of course, there have been reporters. Dozens of reporters!"

"Odd," said Dawlish.

"There's nothing odd about reporters coming here."

"Woman, don't be difficult. Ilott, young Kimble and Carlotta," said Dawlish. "Did you say that Ilott claimed to have known Carlotta in Prague, Ted?"

"Before the war. She couldn't have been more than a kid."

Felicity said: "Carlotta Morlay isn't as young as she looks. She's not far off thirty, but looks twenty-one. She'll probably look thirty when she's fifty, she has that kind of face and figure. Do you trust her, Pat?"

"What does your feminine intuition say?"

"She's very intense," said Felicity. "Continental, if you like. She's obviously had a lot of worry, and she's living on her nerves. Ilott is, too. As for young Kimble . . ." She shrugged her shoulders. "I should say that he's the nearest to a cat on hot bricks I've ever seen. And there was a peculiar thing."

"Hm-hm?" Dawlish's mouth was full of toast.

"He didn't mention his father."

Beresford stirred in his chair, Dawlish wrinkled his nose, and there was a ring at the front-door bell. Felicity went to answer it.

"Fel's got something," said Beresford. "Young Kimble's a bit off the average norm, isn't he? Looks to me like a man with a heavy conscience. Thought much about him?"

"A little." Dawlish finished eating, poured himself out another cup of coffee, and lit a cigarette. He felt fresh and fit enough to tackle anything. His expression was wooden and he didn't speak for some minutes. Felicity had spoken to someone at the door, but hadn't come in, and hadn't given the caller much time.

"Like to brood on your own?" asked Beresford.

Dawlish smiled. "Thanks, Ted. But you're never in the way." He looked wooden. "I'm getting to this, which is glaringly obvious—Trivett probably realized it last night. We can't believe everything we hear of Ilott, Carlotta or young Terry! By the way, how much did you tell Trivett?"

"Everything I know."

"That's everything I know," said Dawlish. "But here's something I guess. Kimble came across this drug by accident and let Mascatti know about it—naturally enough as he was working for Mascatti. Rutter overheard. Rutter saw the chance of a lifetime. As Trivett said, he was working under cover. He got hold of this formula. I wouldn't put it past him to have copied it from the paper which Kimble left down the side of that chair, and left the original with us, to fool us. And we were duly fooled." Dawlish smiled but that didn't really alter the woodenness of his expression. "I wonder if Trivett's working on the same lines." He stood up, stubbed out a cigarette, and went into the other room for the telephone.

Trivett was soon on the line; a brisk and businesslike Trivett.

"Hallo, Pat." He talked and listened for several minutes and then said: "Yes, I was always pretty sure that Rutter was a king-pin. He's always managed to get behind someone else and turn suspicion on them. Mascatti's reputation is irreproachable. He's nearly mad with anxiety, too. His latest is to offer a five thousand pound reward for Rutter's capture. That'll be in the late papers tonight and the early ones in the morning. What he doesn't seem to realize is that Rutter isn't in this on his own. Rutter may have stolen the formula, but he didn't make the stuff himself, he'd need a chemist—and a pretty good one."

"Ah," said Dawlish. "Who?"

"I'm going very closely into the background of this man Ilott," said Trivett.

Dawlish murmured, "Ever thought of Kimble?"

"Well, yes," said Trivett, taking him seriously. "But I doubt if he's as two-faced as that. Can't leave him out, though. Rutter might have wanted him so as to get more of the stuff, too. Kimble may have made some, Rutter took it, ran out, needed more and snatched Kimble, whom he could force to manufacture it. That would let both Ilott and Kimble out. We'll see. Any bright ideas yourself?"

"I'm having even fewer bright ideas than usual," said Dawlish modestly. "Keep in touch, Bill."

Trivett said slowly: "Yes. And listen. We didn't really know what this business was before, so I don't complain that you kept so much to yourself. But don't keep any more. Stop the lone wolf act."

"Yes, sir," murmured Dawlish.

Trivett grunted, and rang off. Dawlish sat back in his chair, looking at the ceiling, unsmiling; and Beresford sat with the patience of Job. The flat was very quiet for several minutes, until Dawlish stretched out for the telephone directory.

"Wonder if young Kimble's in," he said. "Now what's that address? Gaw Road . . ." he ran his forefinger down the Ki's. "Kilson, Kilt . . . Kimack . . . Kimble, here we are, 81234."

He dialled, then put down the receiver briskly.

"We'll go and see Terry," he decided. "And check on Carlotta as we go."

CHAPTER XXIV

TERRY KIMBLE

Roger Brent was sitting at the wheel of a small Morris, a hired car, for his own would be too easily identifiable. He was within sight and easy distance of Carlotta's flat. He was smoking, looking through a sporting paper and, as they approached, they saw him yawn twice. He looked up, and waved.

They drew alongside.

"Busy?" asked Dawlish.

"Oaf. No."

"Has she been out since coming to the flat?"

Brent grinned.

"She hasn't had a lot of chance. Terry Kimble was there just after eleven o'clock. Ilott arrived soon after. Terry left. Then she went out with Ilott, told me she was going to see you, and she did. Truthful minx, isn't she? Ilott brought her back, and hadn't been gone five minutes before young Terry arrived again, looking like violent death. Warmed up," added Brent thoughtfully. "He looked much colder when he left."

Dawlish said thoughtfully, "I wonder why?"

"She's letting Ilott eat out of her hand, and Terry looks more murderous every time he leaves," said Brent. "Believe the obvious."

"What is obvious?" asked Dawlish. "Seen the police?"

"There's a chap at a window across the road, and I've seen him at the Yard," said Brent.

"Good. Follow Carlotta if she leaves, won't you?"

"My dear chap!"

Dawlish grinned, and drove off, but he didn't drive straight to Kimble's house. He turned off the Edgware Road, and hoped that Farningham would be in. Farningham's front door was open, and the waiting-room was crowded, half a dozen poorly-dressed and miserable-looking people were standing in the passage. The surgery door opened, and Farningham said to a little, shrivelled-up woman;

"I don't think there's anything to worry about, Mrs. Sprattley. Come in and see me again in three days' time, and I'll have a report ready for you." He smiled, but looked more tired even than on the previous night. He caught sight of Dawlish, and said: "Hallo, Pat. Are you going to be long?"

"Two minutes, Bill."

"Come in, then." Farningham led the way in, and closed the door, wiping his forehead. "You've had a nice Press." He grinned faintly. "Now what?"

"That formula I gave you."

Farningham said slowly, "What about it?"

"It could be this sleep stuff."

Farningham said: "Yes, I suppose it could. The only way to find out would be to experiment. We'd have to start on rats or rabbits. For Pete's sake, don't ask me to do it. What about asking young Ilott?"

"You can't tell, at a glance?"

"Of course I can't." Farningham drew too deeply on a cigarette.

"You know, Pat, it's not a thing you ought to fool about with privately. Hand it over to Trivett, see what his laboratory boys can do. I've been worrying about it whenever I've had a moment to worry. Intended to ring you up and tell you not to play the fool."

"Right!" said Dawlish. "One other thing. Does young Kimble work with his father?"

"Never heard it said," said Farningham. "I don't know what he does."

"Thanks." Dawlish let himself out.

Dawlish half expected to see the police watching Kimble's house. None was in sight; they were keeping in the background. The ancient two-seater roadster was outside the front door, so Terry was in. Dawlish wanted to know several things about Terry, as well as what work he did for a living.

He rang the bell, and waited with Beresford.

A middle-aged woman opened the door. She looked flustered, and although it was the middle of the afternoon wore an old dress and a dust-cap, from which several locks of dank, grey hair escaped. Her eyes were tired.

"Yes, sir?"

"Is Mr. Terence in?"

"Well, he's in," she said, "but I don't want to disturb him, unless it's very important. He's had such a worrying time lately, and now he has dropped off I think it would be cruel to wake him. I do really." She didn't make any move to let them pass.

"How long has he been asleep?" asked Dawlish slowly.

"Oh, not very long. About an hour, I suppose. He's been rushing about all day, and that—that *chit* of a girl is making it worse for him. The moment I set eyes on her I knew she wouldn't be any good to him. Or any good to anybody, for that matter. Foreign, she is. I—"

"Let me go and see him," said Dawlish. "If he's still asleep, I won't wake him."

"Well, I don't know that he'd like—"

"He won't mind. I'm helping to look for his father."

"Oh, I see. Why, yes, of course." Her eyes brightened. "Your picture's in the paper, isn't it? Ever such a strong face, I remember thinking that when I saw it this morning. I suppose it will be all right, and you'll be *very* quiet, won't you?"

"Very quiet," promised Dawlish.

He felt his heart thumping as he followed her up the stairs. Beresford was just behind him; had Beresford sprung to the same possibility? They reached the landing, and the woman padded along a passage and opened the third door on the left. The house seemed even more rambling than it had by night.

She opened the door gently, and peered in. The room was dark, for the curtains were drawn.

"Pulled them myself," she whispered, "he was so tired. He started to write a letter, then he just lay down and dropped off. I took his shoes off, too." She pointed.

Dawlish stepped into the room which he had judged was Terry's, when he had come here. Terry lay on top of the bed with a sheet over him. His stockinged feet poked out at the foot, one arm was over the sheet, the other underneath. He lay on his back—and he didn't make a sound. Dawlish wished the woman weren't here; she breathed wheezily, and he couldn't tell whether Terry was breathing. His mouth was closed, and in the poor light Dawlish could see the expression of repose.

"Please don't wake him," pleaded the woman.

"Just stand still," said Dawlish. He motioned to Beresford, who went across and pulled one of the curtains. The woman made a silent protest. Dawlish studied the young face in the better light. He couldn't see any sign of movement at chest or lips. He put his fingers on the wrist, which was outside the coverlet, seeking the pulse.

He felt no beating.

He said quietly, "We'd better have more light." He slid his hand beneath Terry's shirt and felt for the heart. The woman caught her breath.

Dawlish felt no movement.

Ted pulled the curtains further.

The woman said in a cracked voice: "What's the matter? What are you doing? What's the matter?"

"Steady," said Dawlish. He looked down at Terry Kimble. Terry had come home, tired out—there was nothing surprising in that, for he had been up half the night. He had gone straight to sleep and he wouldn't wake up.

The woman peered closely—then threw up her hands and screamed. Ted tried to pacify her. The curtains were drawn right back now, and broad daylight spread about the room. In this light, Terry Kimble's hair seemed more ginger than ever. He seemed younger, too.

Dawlish tried to ignore the woman's screaming, and looked about the room. There was a desk in one corner, and some writing-paper on it; a fountain-pen, left as if Terry had been too tired to go on writing. He reached the desk and Beresford gripped the woman's shoulders and helped her out of the room.

Dawlish found an unfinished letter beneath the blotter. It was written in a young, clear hand. It was headed:

To Scotland Yard (Supt. Trivett).

I can't face things any longer. I stole the formula for Rutter. It's my fault Dad's in this mess. Rutter promised Dad wouldn't have any more trouble if I did it. I was scared stiff, too. Dad said he'd go to see Dawlish, and I thought it was a good idea—I meant to tell Dawlish what I'd done, but couldn't bring myself to. Rutter kept saying what he'd do to me, and—and Dad and Carlotta.

I can't go on any longer now, I . . .

It stopped there.

Beresford came into the room, shook his head at another scream from downstairs, and walked across to Dawlish.

"There's another woman down there, she'll be all right. What are you going to do?"

Dawlish handed him the letter.

"Oh," said Beresford, reading. "Confession note. What a mess the young fool got himself into. At last he made a half-hearted attempt to put it right, and didn't damn you in Carlotta's eyes." He shrugged his shoulders. "What a devil of a business this is. Rutter makes son work against father, double-crosses everyone, and—" He stopped. "You'll tell Trivett?"

"About Terry?"

"No. The letter."

"I'm not sure," said Dawlish. "If anyone else had found him, Trivett would have it. Trivett was intended to have it. I'd like to make sure it's Terry's writing. It became obvious last night that Terry was in it, of course; I ought to have come here earlier today." He had seldom looked more bleak.

"Obvious?" Beresford was doubtful.

"One of the things I let ride, thinking I could have a cut at Terry when the time was ripe. You told me, Ted. He wanted to know where his father was, didn't he? Kimble had come in the back way, no one was supposed to know he was back, but Terry asked the question, then hastily said he'd had a 'phone call. That

173

was an afterthought. Damn it, you told me! From that moment, Terry was in. Did he do what he says—help Rutter in order to save his father? And—did he kill himself, or was he killed?

"That note—" began Beresford.

"Could be a suicide note. Could be a note he'd written because he couldn't keep up the game and was going to run for it. And it could have been forged after his murder." Dawlish was brisk, but his expression was still wooden. "I wonder if Ilott and Carlotta have been here this morning. The woman downstairs ought to know. Think we can get any sense out of her?"

"Could try," said Beresford. "Queer thing is that Terry being in seems to give Ilott a better chance of being out. If Terry stole the drug and the formula—"

Dawlish shrugged. They went downstairs, the note carefully folded and placed in an envelope, so that finger-prints couldn't be spoiled. The housekeeper sat in the kitchen, leaning back with a cup of tea by her side.

Terry had received two visitors, just before he had gone to sleep. That *chit* of a foreign girl; and a man who looked foreign, with a beard and wild eyes.

CHAPTER XXV

ILOTT RAVES

Roger Brent was yawning again when Dawlish's car turned into the street. He grinned and waved when he recognized it, and pointed to the house; meaning that Carlotta was still in. Dawlish pulled the Rolls-Bentley up behind him, and they got out.

"Gathering of clans," said Brent. "Tim's just gone off to have a snack—he's missed lunch today, he's been so busy keeping check on Ilott. You should hear him fuming at the police, who don't seem to think it worth while watching Ilott."

"Is Ilott here?"

"Arrived half an hour ago," said Brent. "You should see him. Beard trimmed, you can actually see his collar and tie. Very spruce, too, in what looks like a new suit, and believe it or not, he carried a bunch of roses."

"No!"

"Yes. If ever I've seen a lovelorn swain, it's our Dr. Ilott," said Brent. "Fellow looks too much of a scarecrow to be deep in this. Nothing convinces Tim. This is all part of a deep-laid plot to throw dust in the eyes of the police and the great P.D. *And* the dust is going in, thick and proper."

"So you don't think I'll be welcome."

"Ilott will probably throw you out. But try. We'll be here to pick up the pieces."

"I'll risk it," said Dawlish.

He went into the house. It had a narrow passage and stairs running alongside it, there were hundreds of thousands of similar houses in London. There was a faint smell of polish. On a board fastened to the wall were the names of the tenants; Carlotta Morlay was on the third floor. Dawlish went up, slowly, thoughtfully. So much was obvious, so much was obscure. The 'suicide' note was almost too good to be true.

Ilott's progress with Carlotta didn't seem real. *Was* it progress? Was it ridiculous to think of him turning up, spruce as he could make himself, with a bouquet of roses for Carlotta? It just seemed phoney.

Dawlish tapped at the door.

There was a pause; then Ilott opened the door, aggressively, glared—and drew back.

"Oh. It's *you.*"

"Mind if I come in?"

"I don't suppose it would make any difference if I did," said Ilott, "you seem to barge in and out more or less as you want to. It's Dawlish," he called more loudly, and led the way into the room. Dawlish hadn't been here before. He took one approving glance round, and looked at Carlotta. Carlotta knew nothing of Terry's death—he hoped. So it wasn't surprising that she should look fresh and—happy? He hadn't expected to find her looking like that. Nothing was reasonable about her behaviour but— love at first sight was a peculiar thing.

"Good afternoon," she said. "I'm very glad you're better, Mr. Dawlish."

"Thanks. You look fine."

"Yes," she said. "I feel much better. I suppose it's relief, in a way."

"What kind of relief?" Dawlish found himself almost overbearing, and Ilott wouldn't like it. That was a good reason for becoming even more overbearing. "Dr. Kimble's still missing."

"Oh, yes," said Carlotta, and her eyes became shadowed. "But at least the police know who to look for, and there isn't so much mystery. It can only be a matter of time before the police find the doctor and catch Rutter, surely."

"Possibly," said Dawlish.

"I don't know what you want," Ilott growled, "but if you're coming here to start worrying Carlotta, you can go out again. *I've* made it clear she hasn't anything more to worry about. That's final."

"Oh." Dawlish looked at him levelly. "Mr. Know-All."

"If you come here insulting us, I'll throw—"

"Vernon," said Carlotta, "don't shout, please." She was remarkably calm. "Mr. Dawlish has done a great deal to help, and—"

"Has he? Like to know what it is. Been chasing about after his own tail, as far as I can see. Tell me one thing you've done that'd made any difference to this beastly business. Come on—that's a challenge." Ilott jeered. "You've poked your nose into everyone's business, and all you've done is get yourself put to sleep."

"Last night—" began Carlotta.

"I know; you've told me. He took a chance. *That* doesn't surprise me. Dawlish is one of those brainless oafs without any imagination, who doesn't know the meaning of fear. That doesn't make him a master detective. Come on, Dawlish, tell me one thing you've done to help."

Dawlish said mildly, "I pass."

Ilott snorted.

"There you are, you see! He has to admit it. I don't know

whether everything written about him has been hooey, but in this job he's only made a fool of himself. I don't see that it gives him any right to come worrying us."

"Oh, no," said Dawlish. "No right." He dropped on to a couch; the chairs weren't large enough for him. He stretched out his legs, lit a cigarette and smiled up amiably. "Why did you go to the Golden Shoe last night?"

"To see Carlotta. Had to," Ilott added, and didn't say why.

"You forgot to tell me you were going."

"Well, fancy that," sneered Ilott. "I forgot to tell you."

Dawlish shrugged.

"Carlotta, did Mascatti himself give you that letter to take to Ilott—the offer of work? Or was it Rutter?"

"It was Rutter," Carlotta said. "I didn't type the letter, the morning secretary did. Rutter gave it to me, sealed, but told me what was in it. But Mr. Mascatti knew, he was upset when I told him the answer."

But for that, Dawlish would have doubted whether Mascatti had signed the letter himself.

"Thanks. Ilott—why did you go to the Golden Shoe?"

"I've told you. To see Carlotta."

"You're lying."

Ilott glowered. "You may think you're big enough to stop me from throwing you out, but you could be making a mistake. It's true."

"You went to see Mascatti or Rutter. Which?"

"I went to see Carlotta."

Dawlish said slowly: "All right. Why?"

"To hell with you!" shouted Ilott. "That's my business. Get out of here."

"Not yet," said Dawlish. "Not until I've got the truth out of the two of you."

Ilott's face went dusky red, veins showed up on his forehead and neck. He drew nearer, stood over Dawlish with his hands thrust towards him, the fingers crooked; they were powerful hands, he probably had great strength.

"Get out. Understand? Get *out*. Carlotta's told you the simple truth. If you don't—"

Dawlish stood up, suddenly, startled the man and made him back away, startled Carlotta, who came forward, as if to get between the men. They stood face to face, the girl a foot away from them.

"Listen, Ilott," said Dawlish. "Try to stop losing your temper. Use your mind. Kimble came across this sleep drug. Rutter got a supply of it and you know how he's using it. You decided to accept that job offered by Mascatti and Rutter. On my advice, remember? What kind of work? To make more of the drug? Do you know yet?"

"I haven't the faintest idea," Ilott said more calmly. "I didn't go to the Golden Shoe about that."

"What was your real reason for going?"

Ilott didn't shout or rave any more, but looked at Dawlish almost too calmly. He wasn't exactly dazed but didn't look wide awake. He spoke in a much quieter voice.

"Don't be silly."

Carlotta, watching him closely, took his arm.

"Vernon! What's the matter?"

Ilott said: "Silly idiot. As if he can't see I'm in love with you. Have been—ever since I saw you. Years ago. Little girl, then. Couldn't believe," he was speaking very slowly—"couldn't believe—my eyes." He smiled, and it turned into a yawn. He patted Carlotta's hand gently, and staggered away, put out one hand to support himself against a chair, the other to his forehead. "Don't feel well."

"He's ill," Carlotta said in a choky, frightened voice. "He's ill, he—"

Dawlish gripped the man's arm to save him from falling. Ilott leaned his full weight against him, his eyes almost closed. This wasn't phoney, he was falling asleep in front of their eyes.

Dawlish turned away from the telephone. He'd called Trivett. Carlotta was at the bedroom door, looking at him. Ilott lay on the bed, behind her; her bed. He was too long for it. They had loosened his collar, tie and shoes; he had surprisingly small feet for a tall man.

"The doctor's coming," Dawlish said quietly. "Come over here, Carlotta, you can't do anything yourself for a while."

She moved slowly. Her eyes looked enormous, tragic. He found it hard to believe that she was grieving, before grief was necessary, for a man whom she had known for a few hours. Grief was in her whole body, and in her eyes—grief and shock.

Dawlish put a hand on her arm and drew her towards him, and she stood close, as if glad to shelter against his hugeness from the desperation and despair which caught her.

"I want to help," Dawlish said. "Tell me the truth, Carlotta. You were happy—with him. Why? When did you meet him? What have you been doing? Tell me about it all, because if you don't—" He didn't need to finish.

"Oh, God," she said, "don't let him die."

"When did you meet him?"

She pressed close against Dawlish, as a child might.

"You knew I'd seen him before, but didn't recognize him—he's changed, the beard—oh, it was years ago. He knew me, though, and I remember Father talking about him. He was a brilliant pupil. He worked with Kimble."

She paused. Then:

"It may sound silly. Perhaps it is. From the moment I saw him when I called at his house, he—he mattered."

She stared at the door, and said evenly:

"Will they be long?"

"No. Carlotta, do you know why Mascatti offered him work?"

"No. No—I've tried to find out, but I just don't know."

She closed her eyes.

Dawlish said quietly: "Why did Vernon go to the club last night? Was it to see you?"

"Partly. It was something to do with Terry, too. Terry went to see him, you arranged that. Terry was going to the club, and wanted Vernon with him. Vernon thought it would be wise to go, because Terry told him he expected—sensation. Then they both went to sleep, like everyone else."

"Who were the women they were with?"

"Terry's friends."

"Do you know who they were?"

"No, and it does not matter," said Carlotta. "How can it matter? I—"

The front-door bell rang. She sprang away from him crying, "The doctor!" She had pathetic faith that a doctor could help Ilott, as if she didn't realize that no one knew anything about the drug, and whether he lived or died depended wholly on how much he'd had.

She opened the door.

Mascatti spoke, just out of Dawlish's sight.

CHAPTER XXVI

RUTTER THREATENS

Dawlish moved swiftly across the room and into the bedroom, closed the door so that he could see a little and hear everything, and hoped the girl wouldn't betray him. Disappointment loaded her voice.

"Please, why have you come? Why isn't the doctor—?"

Mascatti didn't let her go on, took her hands and came forward into the room. Dawlish saw his intentness, and wondered what explained it.

"Miss Morlay I—must see Dr. Ilott."

"You can't! He—"

"I must see him, it is desperately important," said Mascatti. His voice was so low-pitched that Dawlish only just caught the words. "I have heard from Rutter."

Carlotta gave a little gasp.

"I must see Dr. Ilott."

"He is ill!"

"I must see him." Mascatti seemed to be gripping her hands tightly enough to hurt. "Rutter has threatened to use the drug again, tonight, to *kill*—unless Dr. Ilott will see him. It is vital. Where is he?"

Dawlish stepped out of the bedroom, Mascatti started, recognized him and came swinging across, hands raised as if in appeal.

"Mr. Dawlish, you can influence Ilott. I have heard from Rutter, an ultimatum. He will use the drug today unless Ilott sees him. You can influence Ilott, and you must."

The girl was by Mascatti's side; hopeless.

Dawlish said slowly: "Yes, I think I could. I can try."

"You must try!"

"But—" began Carlotta.

"Leave this to me, Carlotta," Dawlish said. "When did you hear from Rutter?"

"He telephoned."

"In person?"

"Yes, of course; I recognized his voice. I came straight here, because Dr. Ilott's housekeeper told me that he had come to see Miss Morlay. Is he here now? Is he?"

"He'll be back soon."

"I'll wait for him, perhaps it will help if I—"

"It won't help," Dawlish said. "Where is he to meet Rutter? What has he to do? I'll arrange it, if it can be arranged."

"It must be arranged," said Mascatti. His eyes were blazing. He had the handsomeness of a past age, the manner, the flair. "Dawlish, we don't know how many people will suffer if this fails. You . . ." He caught his breath. "You won't try to trick him. You won't gamble with lives."

"I won't gamble."

Mascatti said abruptly: "I don't think I trust you that far. You would take any chance to capture Rutter. I won't take such a chance. Miss Morlay, seek Ilott, find him, tell him he must come to me at once."

Mascatti swung round on his heel; Dawlish could imagine a cloak swirling from his shoulders, the scabbard of a sword jutting out behind him. Carlotta opened her mouth to scream the truth; Dawlish clapped a hand on her shoulder, silencing her. Mascatti opened the door and went out, closing it quietly behind him.

"Why did you let him go? What are you doing?" Carlotta flung the words out.

Dawlish said, "Rutter will try me, I think, if this fails." His expression was almost as despairing as the girl's. Her eyes were shadowed with desperation, she hurried to the window and looked out, saying nothing until she exclaimed:

"A car!"

There were two cars. Trivett arrived in one, a police-surgeon and another doctor in the other. Carlotta flew at Trivett. Why had he been so long, didn't he realize the gravity of this? Trivett was soothing. Few doctors knew anything about the drug, and he had made sure of getting one who did. Carlotta led the doctors to the bedroom, leaving Trivett and Dawlish together; a grim-faced Trivett.

"Take anything from Terry Kimble, Pat?"

Dawlish said "Yes," and handed over the letter. He talked as Trivett read. "Kick me as hard as you like, but I wanted to see Carlotta and Ilott first. Had an odd idea that I might get more out of them, quickly."

"Did you?"

"Not really."

"Nothing much matters now except finding Rutter and getting Kimble, the rest will sort itself out," Trivett said. "Any ideas?"

"Mascatti has."

Trivett growled: "You've got Mascatti on the brain. He doesn't know a thing more—"

"Easy," said Dawlish, and told him what had happened,

watched Trivett's eyes fill with grim shadows. Trivett had always been worried about this, had seen the possibility that the mystery was connected with the sleeping deaths, had been ready to jump at the chance of help from Dawlish. Now Trivett was at his wit's end; had been fighting shadows and was still fighting them.

He said, "I'll deal with Mascatti."

"Give Rutter a chance to tackle me."

"What makes you think he will?"

"I've given Mascatti plenty of time to think about it. Now I'll convince him I can make Ilott play. He'll tell Rutter—"

Trivett said slowly, "Meaning that Rutter knows he can't do a deal with us, but thinks he might fix one with you."

"That's it," said Dawlish. "I tried to sell Mascatti and him a pup, early on. I think Rutter bought it. He probably thinks I'll play, for sufficient money."

"It could happen. He knows Mascatti well, and tried what seemed the easier way." Trivett looked towards the bedroom door, but as Dawlish moved to the outer door, called, "Pat."

"Yes?"

Carlotta, who had been staring out of the window, turned and watched them; and her agony was in her eyes.

"What do you know that you're keeping back?" Trivett asked *sotto voce*. "And don't tell me there's nothing. You've kept it to yourself since the beginning."

Dawlish looked inane.

"No, Bill. A guess or two, that's all. Guesses aren't any good to policemen." He went across to Carlotta and took her hands. "Don't worry too much, Carlotta, I think they'll pull him through." He didn't think so, but he had to say something to cheer her. He felt sure that he had heard everything she could tell him. The game had passed her, now—but hadn't passed Ilott.

Dawlish found himself smiling tensely as he drove fast towards the West End. He reached the Golden Shoe just after seven o'clock. Two policemen stood outside and there was a little crowd of sightseers; that was all that was left of the sensation. A newsboy, scenting buyers, was at a nearby corner, shouting:

"Sleepy Death—Latest." He held a paper out to Dawlish, who ignored it and went in. There was no commissionaire on duty; no sultry girl. The inside door was wide open. He went up, and glanced into the empty dining-room. He hadn't seen it when everyone had been sleeping; and in daylight it had a tawdry look. He went up to Mascatti's outer door, opened it without tapping, and strode in.

No one was in the office. The communicating door was open, and Mascatti was sitting at his big desk. Everything had been put back in its proper position, there was little evidence of the fighting.

Mascatti looked up.

"Dawlish!"

"Hallo," said Dawlish casually, and dropped into a chair. "How's your friend Rutter?"

"My *friend*! I would give half my fortune to catch that man."

"You employed him."

Mascatti said bitterly: "Yes, I employed him. I was fool enough to believe that I could handle him. I touched the fringes of the underworld, and look what has happened." He picked up a newspaper. "Two more people have died, in Birmingham. Three more died and others are on the danger list, in London—people who came here last night. The total value of the money and jewels taken is over twelve thousand pounds, as far as can be estimated. And—Kimble is still missing. Do you understand what that means, Dawlish? The man who could do untold good, the man who—"

"Discovered the sleepy death," said Dawlish.

"That was by accident! Dawlish, listen to me. Rutter wants Ilott. He won't be satisfied without him. He telephoned me again after I returned. If you can persuade Ilott to see him—"

"I'll try," said Dawlish. "When Rutter gets in touch with me."

"He'll never be such a fool."

"When he rings up again, just give him the message," said Dawlish. "We'll talk business. I'm going to my flat—the mews flat. I'll wait in until ten o'clock. And tell Rutter I'll do business with him."

He went out, without looking round. He guessed that Mascatti was staring after him. He looked neither right nor left, but hurried down the stairs. The crowd outside had grown larger, several people cried, "There's Dawlish." He pushed past them to the car, and drove off. Ten minutes later he was at the flat. No one came to the window, no one opened the door. He thought nothing of that as he hurried up the steps and let himself in.

"Fel!" he cried.

They were all there: Felicity, Beresford, Jeremy and Brent. Felicity was in one of the huge armchairs, chin on her chest, asleep. The others were asleep too.

CHAPTER XXVII

SECOND FIDDLE

Dawlish moved slowly from Felicity's chair to the telephone, picked up the receiver and, watching her, dialled the Yard. It seemed to be a long time answering. Trivett was back in his office.

"Yes, Pat?"

"Same doctors, same trouble, the flat," Dawlish said stiffly. "Felicity. All of them. See to it, please."

He put down the receiver, hesitated, went across and pressed his hand against Felicity's cool, white forehead. He could see the slight movement of her lips. He took no notice of the others; there was nothing he could do. He went downstairs. A man was cleaning a car at one of the garages. He gave him the key of the flat.

"The police will soon be here. Let them in," he said.

He took the wheel of the Rolls-Bentley, and drove off. He didn't drive fast; certainty was ten times more important than speed. He felt certain of the truth, only doubted how to force it into the open. He reached the Golden Shoe, and the same newsboy offered him a paper, looked at his eyes, and snatched the paper away.

"Sorry, Guv'nor."

One of the little crowd peering at the open door said, "Look, there's that man Dawlish." A murmur of conversation followed; and as Dawlish drew nearer faded into silence. He went in and up the stairs; there was silence.

Mascatti's door was ajar.

He opened the door slowly and quietly, and Mascatti was still at work at the desk, apparently absorbed in it. He went closer, and Mascatti saw his shadow, stiffened and glanced up. He put the pen down, slowly, and stood up.

"Dawlish, what is the trouble?"

Dawlish said: "My wife's the trouble. I want Rutter."

"But—"

Dawlish said: "Listen, Mascatti. I want Rutter and you know how to contact him. You know, don't lie to me. He may have you under his thumb, he may have frightened you into doing what he wants. I'll frighten you more. I want Rutter and I want him now."

Mascatti backed away.

"Dawlish, you don't understand what you're doing. I told him about you and Ilott. He says he wants Ilott, you—you have to produce him. He threatened to attack your wife if you didn't—"

"He attacked her too soon."

Mascatti moistened his lips. "It's—difficult for you. Personal. I can see it in terms of others. Dozens, perhaps hundreds of others. He's threatened to use the drug mercilessly, unless you produce Ilott."

"Well, he's made another mistake. Ilott's got sleepy sickness, too. So he can't have Ilott yet. I want Rutter, and I want him now."

"It's impossible! I can't—"

Dawlish thrust out his right hand, caught Mascatti by the coat lapel, held him tightly and drew him slowly forward, until they were only a foot away from each other.

"I want Rutter. Get him. Or I'll beat you to pulp."

"I can't—"

Dawlish let him go, and hit him—and as he struck he knew that he might be wrong, that this might be a waste of time. Mascatti staggered to one side, knocked against a chair and fell to the floor. He picked himself up, slowly, touched his chin where Dawlish had hit him, looked dazed and sick.

"Hurry," Dawlish said.

Mascatti muttered: "You're making a dreadful mistake, Dawlish. There's too much at stake, this is above personal issues. Be patient. When Rutter gets in touch with me, I'll tell him; I'll try."

"No," said Dawlish. "Listen. If you don't—"

He broke off, at a sound behind him. He moved, swift as a flash, so that his back was towards the wall, and his right hand dropped to his coat pocket. He didn't know whom to expect; certainly not Trivett.

Mascatti muttered: "Superintendent, Dawlish has lost his senses, he thinks I can find Rutter. His wife's ill, he isn't sane. He—"

"I heard what he said." Trivett moved nearer Mascatti, as if prepared to fend Dawlish off if he came to attack again. "I know what's happened. Mascatti, Rutter's blackmailing you. He's always blackmailed you."

Mascatti breathed as if he had been physically hurt.

"There's no other explanation of why you've let him work for you and shelter behind you," Trivett said. His glance at Dawlish seemed to say, 'I can't understand why you haven't realized this.' He went on: "Never mind why he was able to blackmail you. You've a past—but it needn't be brought up against you. Whatever the reason, it isn't strong enough to serve now. If Dawlish is right and you know where Rutter is, tell me."

"He knows," Dawlish said; and he had never felt less like himself, never more like murder.

Mascatti cried: "I don't know! He'll get in touch with me, that's all! And what good will it do Dawlish? If his wife's ill with this sleepy sickness, there's nothing Rutter or anyone else can do about it. There's no antidote, either she'll live or die, it depends how much of the drug she had. Forcing Rutter into the open won't help her, but if we let him have Ilott we might save hundreds of people. Thousands!"

Trivett said abruptly, "Rutter didn't telephone you."

"That's right," Dawlish said. "I couldn't believe you'd let anything through, Bill, so that made Mascatti a liar."

Mascatti put out his hands, as if to fend off a blow.

Trivett went on quietly:

"All the telephone wires here have been tapped. You haven't had any telephone call. I've kept my men out of sight, hoping to bring Rutter into the open. You're protecting him for your own safety. Where is he?"

"You don't understand!" cried Mascatti, "I'm not interested in what happens to me, only in what might happen to others. You've *seen* people die from this drug. Rutter can become a mass murderer, he's not sane. We've got to humour him. If you can't see that, you're a fool. I don't blame Dawlish, he hasn't his wits about him, he's too worried, but you—you can take a dispassionate view of it. Rutter's too powerful for us, we must let him have what he wants. Later you can catch him, but now—"

"Shut up," said Dawlish. "Bill, we'll have to break the place up. Get the walls down. I hoped Mascatti would make it the easy way, but he won't."

Trivett said slowly, "Meaning that Rutter's—"

"Here, of course. Somewhere close to the office. It screams at you. Steel door there—steel door there." He pointed. "The place is like a strong-room, and not just because of the valuables Mascatti keeps in the safe. There's a hiding-place behind one of the walls." He rubbed his nose slowly. "Might be better to start burning the place, that would smoke Rutter out."

"No!" cried Mascatti. "No, you can't—"

"Burn or break them down, I don't mind," said Dawlish. "In fact"—he gave a queer, strangled laugh—"I came prepared." He took a small tin from his pocket, and tossed it in the air. "High explosive." He opened the tin, so that the others couldn't see inside. He closed it again. "All set, now. Which wall shall I start on?" He raised the tin as if to toss it, and Mascatti cried:

"Stop him!"

He moved forward; Trivett stayed where he was. Dawlish dropped his right hand to his pocket and took out the gun. "Keep back, Mascatti. There's one thing I forgot to tell you. My wife *died*. Understand? *Died*. So I don't mind dying and taking you with me. You'd better get out, Bill. I'm going to throw it. Enough here to blow this room and the top of the house into little pieces." He threw back his head and laughed again; the sound echoed through the room, like the laughter of a madman. "Hurry, Bill!"

He made a tossing motion with the tin again.

Mascatti gave a little moaning sound.

"No," he said. "No. I'll—show you. But be careful, be careful, Rutter has a spray of the drug, he can—"

"We'll chance it," Dawlish said.

He stood with the tin in one hand and the gun in the other. Trivett seemed to have forgotten that he was a policeman; that he was here. Mascatti went slowly to the wall, behind the desk. His hands were trembling, and sweat beaded his fine forehead.

His fingers moved along the panelling, then the forefinger pressed.

He turned round, slowly—then quickened his pace, towards the wall away from Dawlish.

Part of the wall was moving—sliding to one side; and they could see through into another room. Mascatti stood close to the wall as the door opened further—and Mascatti had his right hand in his pocket. The door was open a foot. Mascatti spoke in a low-pitched, frantic voice:

"I won't let him get you, I'll try to stop him, I've asked for this." The door was open nearly eighteen inches, he could squeeze through. He took a step forward—and as he moved, Dawlish leapt. Dawlish reached him and thrust him aside. He staggered away, right hand coming from his pocket and the gun showing in it.

Dawlish saw Rutter, gun in hand, standing at the far side of a small room. Kimble—sitting in an easy chair, apparently asleep.

"Be careful!" screamed Mascatti. "Dawlish!" He leapt forward, thudded into Dawlish, had a fury of strength which actually shifted the giant. He levelled his gun. Dawlish shot out a hand and struck it aside, then fired at Rutter's right arm.

Rutter fired.

Rutter's bullet caught Mascatti in the shoulder, Dawlish's caught Rutter in the arm. Rutter's gun dropped. He bent down to get it, and Dawlish fired again, hit the gun and sent it sliding across the wooden floor. Mascatti was groaning.

Trivett reached Dawlish.

"Enough, Pat."

"Oh, yes," said Dawlish, and laughed; and it was no longer the laughter of a madman. "Quite enough, it's all over bar the shouting. Go and get your Rutter." Trivett went into the small room, and Dawlish looked at the tin from his pocket, and laughed again.

CHAPTER XXVIII

THE SHOUTING

Mascatti leaned against the wall, one hand clutching his wounded shoulder, his body drooping. A policeman joined him, and helped him to take his coat off, another went to Rutter, who had no fight left in him. Dawlish and Trivett hurried to Kimble.

Kimble was asleep.

Dawlish went back into the room, and spoke quietly to Mascatti.

"So Rutter blackmailed you into letting him stay here."

Mascatti said: "Yes. Yes, that's true." There was no life in his voice.

"How long has he been blackmailing you?"

"It started—last night. After the raid. I didn't even know he knew about my—my own past." Mascatti straightened up, looked at Trivett, and spoke more firmly. "That will have to come out, I think I'm glad. I've tried to prevent it. I suspected that Rutter was working against Kimble, but I made a fatal mistake—I thought he was an underling, serving another master. I tried to find out who the master was. I was wrong."

"What do you know now?" asked Dawlish.

"Everything, I think," said Mascatti. "He's been frightened, frightened men talk." He watched the police giving Rutter first aid, and ignored the man who was tending his own wound—which wasn't serious. "It began when I asked for Kimble's help with the drug I told you about. Kimble was often here, and Rutter searched his house one day. He found that most of the work that was supposed to be Kimble's own was actually another man's—a dead man's. Kimble let it be thought that it was his own. Don't ask me how Rutter found out—he did. He began to blackmail Kimble.

"I knew nothing of it.

"Then Kimble stumbled across the sleeping drug, in his synthetic plasma experiments, and told me about it. Rutter overheard, and saw the foul use that could be made of the drug. He tried to get the formula and some supplies from Kimble, who wouldn't part with them, but Kimble's mind was failing, he had blank periods, he wasn't a good risk. Rutter got what he wanted from Terry Kimble, but he couldn't make the drug, and had only limited supplies. He needed another man to work for him, but worked cleverly in with my own plans.

"I knew I couldn't rely on Kimble much longer, and I needed help with the serum I told you about. I tried to get Ilott's help. You know what happened, and how Rutter killed Percy Dipper and left the body at Ilott's place, took a photograph, and then tried to blackmail Ilott. Ostensibly, Ilott would have been working for me, actually for Rutter.

"It was Rutter who sent Dipper and Dipper, hating me, named me. Rutter got your friend drunk, who tried the same trick on you. You were becoming dangerous. He kidnapped your wife."

Mascatti paused.

A doctor came in, and took over from the police.

Dawlish said gently, "Go on, Mascatti."

"Rutter was leading a big gang, and lacked some of the qualities he needed. He knew he must have much more of the sleep drug, to get really big results, but instead of working only for that, he got cold feet. He used what he had, here and at Birmingham, so as to cash in while he could, and it proved his big mistake."

"I see," said Dawlish quietly.

"There's little else," said Mascatti. "He wasn't capable of using the gas or the drug properly—he actually tried it out on his own men. But on some it had a delayed action effect—as it had with a man named Scotty, whom he used. He killed Dipper with the stuff, too.

"After the raid here, he went into hiding. I didn't know, at first. When I was here alone, he came out and talked to me. Many years ago—twenty-five years ago, Dawlish—I operated a big fence's organization in Italy. Rutter knew it, but I didn't know that he knew. I made a fortune. I—well, why not use the word?—I retired. You can say I was repentent, if you like. I'd seen this disease I told you about killing thousands of people in Italy, and I spent a fortune trying to find a cure. Kimble found it.

"When Rutter faced me with my past, I was thunderstruck. I did what he asked—he still clung to the idea of getting Ilott's help with the drug. Kimble is useless now. Rutter didn't realize that until last night. Rutter seemed to think that possession of the drug would make him all-powerful. You know what happened. But as time passed and I realized what was at stake, I tried to gain time and save myself from the past, but—I wouldn't have let Rutter live. I would have killed him. In fact," Mascatti added with strange dignity, "I wish you had let me shoot him."

Dawlish actually smiled.

"As well I didn't. I'll be surprised if they hold your past against you." He moved away, and winked at Trivett. "Bill, you're the

most patient policeman I know. Thanks. Your turn now. Oh—
do you think they'll use Mascatti's past against him?"

"Not if the rest is true," said Trivett.

"Oh, it's true," said Mascatti, and there was a glow, as of hope,
in his eyes.

The police took Rutter, Mascatti and Kimble to hospital—but
when Kimble arrived he was dying.

During the day the police found the papers which proved
that he had been living for years in another man's glory and
trying desperately to be worthy of it.

They learned other things, too. Rutter's men had broken into
the mews flat and taken Kimble away, knowing that Kimble
was prepared to tell Dawlish everything and could no longer
be blackmailed into silence. Kimble, in one of his periods of
complete sanity, had left his wallet behind, giving the secret of
the sleeping drug. On the evening of the big raid Kimble had
come round. He was held in a small flat. He was believed to be
helpless, unable to move, and his guard was careless. Kimble
simply walked out. He did not remember what had happened,
except the quarrel with Mascatti, and he went to make it up.
Rutter knew that if he had a period of clearheadedness he could
give everything away. Rutter had to get him back.

The second raid at the mews flat had been made through a
fanlight, and gas had been sprayed into the room, strong enough
to put Felicity and the three men to sleep. No one yet knew what
had happened to Ilott; but he was on the mend.

The little stock of the gas and the drug, which Rutter still had,
was found in the room where he had been hiding.

There were photographs of Carlotta, too. When Dawlish
puzzled over some of Rutter's tactics, he knew that Rutter had
been infatuated by the girl; had taken chances—like following

her to Victoria—because of her, which had brought the end nearer.

Rutter hadn't been big enough for the task he undertook. At moments his courage ran out. He had kidnapped Felicity, sent the warning photograph; then sensed what Dawlish would do if Felicity were hurt. So he'd sent her back, believing a threat of 'I'll do it again' would put Dawlish off. In the end he'd blamed Dawlish for the impending disaster; in a vicious fit of malice, he had attacked Felicity and the others in the mews flat.

Next day Felicity and Dawlish were packing the one case they had opened at the flat. Beresford had gone; Brent had telephoned. Tim Jeremy was out, but would be back at any moment. The Dawlishes had lazed all the morning, and in the largest armchair was every daily newspaper; each had spread itself on the end of the Sleepy Death crimes. Two ran leaders, demanding that the formula be destroyed; for once Dawlish agreed with newspaper editorials.

Felicity stopped folding a dress, took his hand, examined it earnestly, and let it fall.

"Looking forward to pigs and apples and orchards and dust?" Dawlish asked.

"Darling," said Felicity, "if there's one place I want to go, it's home. I've almost forgotten Paris, but—"

"It'll be a long time before I forget the models," said Dawlish ruefully. "It'll take months to restore the bank balance. Yes, it was worth it," he added hastily, "I'll just pop into the kitchen—"

"You will stop here and help me pack," said Felicity firmly.

"Pooh! Fancy wanting help with a little job like that. I thought you could do with a cup of tea." He glanced at the door, and the front-door bell rang. "Not Tim," he said, "he has a key. I won't be a jiffy."

He went out; Felicity continued folding—and then stopped, for she heard his voice at its heartiest and recognized the ring of genuine pleasure in it.

"Hallo, there! Come in, come in. Fel!"

Felicity went to the passage, and saw Carlotta and Ilott; a radiant Carlotta and a spruce Ilott. If he put on a little more flesh, Felicity reflected, Ilott would be good-looking. She wondered what he was like without his beard.

They went into the big room.

"Mr. Trivett told us you were leaving London and we wanted to come and say good-bye," said Carlotta.

"Nice of you both," beamed Dawlish. "Feel in a talkative mood, Ilott?"

Ilott smiled broadly. "No."

"I thought you wouldn't. But tell me this—how did you get dosed with that damned stuff?"

Carlotta said quickly, "Because he is a fool, and I have made him promise not to do things like it again."

"Like what?"

"Well," said Ilott, "any fool with eyes in his head could have seen that the sleepy death drug was connected with the blood plasma research, so I experimented. Took some of my by-product myself, and it had a delayed action effect. I thought I'd got the formula wrong, or else I hadn't taken enough of it, but it caught up on me at a bad time. There's only one thing to be sorry about, it worried Carlotta."

"Never worry, Carlotta," said Dawlish. "That's a cardinal rule in life. And what now?"

Ilott beamed.

"We're going to get married, of course—quite soon. As soon as I've finished a little job. Nearly done, as a matter of fact." He was airy. "The synthetic plasma should become a reality. Kimble was pretty near, and I'm carrying on where he left off. I'm pretty sure the stuff will turn out all right. When it's on the market commercially, we'll be able to live quite comfortably."

Dawlish laughed.

"Money-grabbing parasite," he said.

"That's right," said Ilott.

ABOUT THE AUTHOR

John Creasey, born in 1908, was a paramount English crime and science fiction writer who used myriad pseudonyms for more than six hundred novels. He founded the UK Crime Writers' Association in 1953. In 1962, his book *Gideon's Fire* received the Edgar Award for Best Novel from the Mystery Writers of America. Many of the characters featured in Creasey's titles became popular, including George Gideon of Scotland Yard, who was the basis for a subsequent television series and film. Creasey died in Salisbury, UK, in 1973.

THE PATRICK DAWLISH MYSTERIES

FROM OPEN ROAD MEDIA

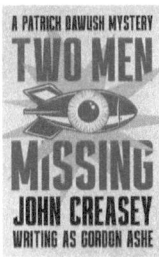

OPEN ROAD

INTEGRATED MEDIA

Find a full list of our authors and
titles at www.openroadmedia.com

FOLLOW US
@OpenRoadMedia

EARLY BIRD BOOKS

FRESH DEALS, DELIVERED DAILY

Love to read?
Love great sales?

Get fantastic deals on
bestselling ebooks delivered
to your inbox every day!

Sign up today at
earlybirdbooks.com/book

www.ingramcontent.com/pod-product-compliance
Lightning Source LLC
Chambersburg PA
CBHW050326110726
47899CB00007B/2394